WHAT OTHERS ARE SAYING ABOUT THIS BOOK

"After I picked this book up I couldn't put it down. I got it stuck to my claw."

> – Peaches Poomer, *Park Bear*

"Finally, Winnie the Pooh for grownups."

> – B.R. Graves, *good friend of Pete*

"Ralph is such a windbag I never liked him much, but this is hard hitting *flux de bouche* ... tells the Bear story like it really is ... riveting. Merrill has set the standard by which all future Bear stuff must be measured. Two thumbs up."

> – Purple Lips Bartley,
> (send check c/o *The Kamilche Ursine Times*)

"Awesome book, dude, way cool."

> – Macduff Shakesbear, *close relative of Ralph*

"This book reduces lateral buckling to insignificance."

> – P. Halvorsen, *Pete's son-in-law*

"Will this sort of frippery never end?"

> – Wm. Shakespeare, *author*

"I told that old geezer not to write this stuff about me."

> – Ralph, *himself*

"What book?"

> – Larry Gordon, *Pete's neighbor*

RALPH

• Conversations With A Bear •

BY PETE MERRILL

Pete Merrill

SECOND EDITION 2003

Printed in Victoria, Canada

This is a work of fiction. Names, characters and incidents are the products of the author's imagination or are used fictitiously. Any resemblance to actual persons, living or dead, is entirely coincidental.

Peter A. Merrill, Sr.
14103 E. Highway 106
Belfair, WA 98528

ISBN 0-935693-20-3
SECOND EDITION 2003

Cover design and book production by Pam Merrill
Outlook Writing & Design - Belfair

National Library of Canada Cataloguing in Publication Data

Merrill, Pete
        Ralph : conversations with a bear / Pete Merrill.

ISBN 1-4120-1167-1

        1. Bears—Fiction.   I. Title.

PS3613.E776R34 2004   813'.6   C2003-904686-9

TRAFFORD

This book was published *on-demand* in cooperation with Trafford Publishing.
On-demand publishing is a unique process and service of making a book available for retail sale to the public taking advantage of on-demand manufacturing and Internet marketing.
On-demand publishing includes promotions, retail sales, manufacturing, order fulfilment, accounting and collecting royalties on behalf of the author.

Suite 6E, 2333 Government St., Victoria, B.C. V8T 4P4, CANADA

Phone	250-383-6864	Toll-free	1-888-232-4444 (Canada & US)
Fax	250-383-6804	E-mail	sales@trafford.com
Web site	www.trafford.com	TRAFFORD PUBLISHING IS A DIVISION OF TRAFFORD HOLDINGS LTD.	
Trafford Catalogue #03-1545	www.trafford.com/robots/03-1545.html		

10   9   8   7   6   5   4   3   2

To Pam, Melinda and Betty

Bear up when the load is heavy
Bear down when the going gets tough
Bear the burden when you think it need be
But for God's sake – don't burden the bear
We've got enough trouble already.

– Ralph Beauregard Shakesbear

Introduction

After I hung up my chalk and eraser, ending twenty-two years of labor in the vineyards of secondary education, I realized that in my retirement I would need to find some means of keeping my mental and physical senses stimulated. The experts in the field call this "keeping busy," and to the average red-blooded American male, keeping busy means "taking up golf." Mark Twain rightly characterized golf as "the ruination of a good walk," and I was determined to avoid it. Instead, I took up woodcarving, which when I consider the mischief this hobby eventually got me into, was probably just as bad.

The return to woodcarving was really only the resumption of a hobby I had begun as a boy of thirteen or so, when I had badgered my mother into buying me a little set of carving tools. I had been smitten at an early age by what the art crowd describes as the "creative muse." I discovered that I could fashion small objects in wood and offer them as gifts to family and friends on special occasions back in those hard scrabble depression years when cash to buy presents at the five and dime store was hard to come by.

I practiced this hobby off and on through the usual forty or fifty years of a checkered career, involving four moves, six different occupations, and a family of five children, all culminating in those aforementioned twenty-two years of teaching.

At last came retirement, and suddenly I had all kinds of time on my hands. I still had the little carving set along with scads of more expensive tools and once again, I felt the tug of artistic fulfillment. So I built a little shop on the highway across from my house and set about "keeping myself busy." I became a woodcarver, first just to amuse myself and, then, as so often happens, the word spread, and I went from giving my creations away to having people stand in line to pay real money for them. I went through several creative phases, each increasing in complexity and in size, until I eventually ended up using a noisy chainsaw to attack large logs of cedar, maple and fir, all in the pursuit of those creative muses that wouldn't seem to leave me alone.

And this brings me to the story I want to tell you.

It was in this thicket that I first met Ralph way back in 1990. You can be sure he was in there, but you would have had to look sharp to find him, he was always very evasive.

Some years ago I met a bear up in the woods behind my house. He was very secretive and he made me swear that I wouldn't tell anybody about his existence. But the statute of limitations on my promise is about to run out and now that we know each other better, he said he guessed it would be okay for me to tell you about him, as long as I don't let on exactly where he lives.

His name is Ralph; it took me a long time to figure that out because bears have trouble with pronunciation and each time I'd ask him his name, it seemed to come out different – it sort of sounded like he was barking. For a long time I called him just "Bear" which seemed to be all right with him, and then one day he mentioned that his mother had actually given him a name, which led us to the business about the pronunciation. We settled on "Ralph" as being close enough.

Ralph is a black bear and he's a big one – probably weighs more than 300 pounds – but he's light on his feet, as are most bears, and contrary to what you might believe, he doesn't smell bad expect for a short time during rutting season. This isn't usually a problem because it isn't a good idea to be hanging around bears during rutting season, anyway. Ralph is a smart bear, though not nearly as smart as he thinks he is. Until you get to know a bear pretty well, it's not a good idea to keep telling him he doesn't know what he's talking about.

I realize that there are plenty of people who refuse to believe that animals can talk, but take my word for it, some animals are quite literate. Years ago I used to have regular conversations with a cow. Talking with a cow has severe limitations, too, since, if I may be forgiven for saying so, cows are not very smart and all this old cow wanted to talk about was how much she disliked cats. Ralph is not only literate, he is opinionated and very outspoken.

Bears don't actually talk so much as they mumble, which makes them difficult to understand. My problem with Ralph was that when I first met him he couldn't write, or at least he said he couldn't, and since the deal I made with him required a lot of writing, it caused me considerable inconvenience. I learned to put up with it though, and eventually we got it worked out.

By the way, cows are also hard to understand because they always talk with their mouths full.

Ralph's philosophy in a nutshell.

CHAPTER ONE

Into the Thicket

The shop, showing that awful hill in the background, which is much steeper than it appears in the photo. That's Ralph on the left holding his sign. The other folks have been waiting there for the arrival of the stagecoach since 1986. They are very patient.

In the summer of 1990, I was standing outside my little shop on Highway 106 in Belfair, looking at a big cedar log and wondering what to do with it. Since the artistic juices didn't seem to be flowing that day, there was a great temptation to just get out the chainsaw and make some kindling. I know lots of people who would do just that and there was a time when I would have too, back when keeping warm was more important than being artistic. But this was a fine specimen of timber – straight grain, no knots, nicely seasoned, six feet long and twenty-eight inches in diameter. I knew there was a creature of some sort in there demanding to get out, but I didn't know yet what it was. Don't be puzzled by that last sentence, I'm just using some of that special jargon artists use to confound lay people into believing what they do is beyond the understanding of just regular folks like you. Stuff like "voices emanating from within their chosen medium giving tangible expression to their unconscious urges," or "discovering the basic interconnectedness of the artist with the more ethereal elements of his universe."

This is obfuscation, the artistic equivalent of how a politician talks when he wants to avoid answering a question. Well, fine, but I'm not that kind of artist. There's no obfuscation here; no flimflam either. What I do is take a piece of wood and whittle or hack at it until it turns into something recognizable and if it doesn't, well, it all burns nicely in the stove. But there's no question that it helps to know what you want to end up with before you begin work. This is especially helpful when you're going to tackle a fine big chunk of wood like the one I was standing there looking at. Without a definite goal you will surely end up with a small log and a large pile of sawdust, a waste of both time and logs.

I knew that this cedar was 93 years old, give or take a few, because while awaiting the arrival of those inner urges, I sat down and counted the annual rings and discovered that about the time this tree was a sprout, Teddy Roosevelt was charging up San Juan Hill. That cedar tree had hardly gotten a good start in life – had barely reached adolescence – when it was struck down in 1989 by the affliction that carries off so many of its kind: "Sudden Chainsaw Death Syndrome" or, as it is known in modern acronymical jargon, SCDS. I don't want the gentle reader to think that *I* cut this tree down. Heavens NO! It was given to me by someone who found it to be an inconvenience wherever it was growing, sawed it down (the work of but a moment nowadays) and gave the butt of it to me knowing that I used such things in my work.

Nothing was happening with the inner voices. Nothing but silence issued from the depths of the log. The muses were still.

"I think what we are facing here," I remarked to myself, "is a clear-cut case of carver's block, the woodland equivalent of the dreaded writer's block." (When the creative urgings fail me, I often resort to conversations with myself.)

What my other self said to me at this point was "Why don't you go up the hill and see if the berries are ripe?"

"Might as well," I said. "I'm not getting any artistic inspiration standing around here."

Listening for the inner voices.

It had been an unusually warm spring and there was a chance of a good crop of wild blackberries if we were to get a reasonable amount of rain at the right time. I hadn't been up the hill to check things out for a considerable time, since getting up there requires too much effort. This is an extremely steep hill and I'm surprised that the whole thing hasn't long since slid down on top of my shop, which is right at the bottom of it. The "permanent angle of repose," as the engineers call it, is close to sixty degrees, making it a major undertaking to scramble to the top, which is about 200 feet up. At the time I'm talking about, the upland property was pretty much a tangled wasteland, since the developers hadn't gotten there yet to lay waste to what was once our very own private wilderness. This was also before I built the switchback trail, which I'll tell you about later.

By the time I had struggled to the top through the huckleberry thickets, snags, brambles and mountain beaver burrows I was exhausted. I perched on a stump just outside the blackberry patch to do some heavy breathing. This berry patch was a big one, far larger than the usual run-of-the-mill variety we have around here. It had been growing larger year-by-year, and now spread out to encompass over half an acre and was clearly in good health since the berries were very nearly ripe. Good berry patches require lots of sun, so they usually appear in cutover land. This area had been logged some years earlier and was now in prime condition, but there was still enough underbrush and new-growth timber to make it a very secluded place, seemingly quite isolated, yet closer to civilization than a stranger would believe.

Now I had to find a way through the brambles to check out the interior and it's no easy task to get into these thickets. Brer Rabbit knew what he was doing when he chose a briar patch for a sanctuary. I had scrambled but a short way around the patch when I came upon what appeared to be a well-defined trail into the interior. Dang, I thought to myself. Somebody's been in here ahead of me. Likely some of the old folks from over at that new residential development scouting out the territory.

I knew it had to be old folks because young folks don't pick wild blackberries. Hardly anyone young picks anything any more. It's too

4

much work and it's too hard to get them away from the TV and the Nintendo games. Most old folks, on the other hand, look forward to picking wild stuff. I think it reminds them of the depression when they were sent out into the woods to collect "vittles" without which they probably had "slim pickins" or something similar. We old folks spend a lot of time talking about things like that.

Well, anyway, there's no question that there was a path to the interior of the patch right there in front of me and it spared me the trouble of making one for myself. Maybe some of those old folks were in there right now and we could discuss a division of the crop, rather than get into a territorial dispute later on. One year when the crop was meager, I had a heated discussion with another picker, a guy named Elbert or Ethelbert, about who was trespassing on whose private territory. The berries I'm talking about aren't on my property and they weren't on his either, so neither of us had "legal standing." We settled the matter amicably without bloodshed, but you can get an idea what a big deal these things are around here.

It's spooky going into a place like that. The brambles were higher than my head, making this a mighty dense piece of real estate, impossible to see through and harder to negotiate than the razor wire at the state penitentiary. Had it not been for that trail leading into the interior I think I would have given up then and there.

And speaking of the trail, it was beginning to look less and less like it was made by people and more and more like the work of critters. Critters, yeah, but what kind of critters? Pretty big critters, I thought. Please remember that I was up there all alone in that remote place with only myself to talk to. My imagination began to take over, like in one of those old Disney movies full of foreboding, gloomy forests where all the trees have sinister eyes and evil grins and bats flap about. I was beginning to think maybe it was time to go back down the hill and talk to that log.

I was perhaps twenty feet into the thicket, when I heard the sound that froze me in my tracks. There was no mistaking it, and it wasn't the sound made by any gaggle of old geezers picking berries. From just around the next turn in the trail came a loud snuffle, a sound that literally turned my blood to water. I know there is only one creature in the whole animal kingdom that snuffles.

BEARS SNUFFLE!

Now, around here we have just one kind of bear, that being the North American Black Bear (*Ursus americanus*), who much prefers the company of other bears to people (*Homo sapiens*). As a matter of fact, I'm told that when a black bear encounters a human, even one as non-threatening as I am, his first instinct is to "get out of town." While this was flashing through my brain I was also thinking that if there was only one way out of "town" – that being the way I came in – then me and this bear dude were apt to be using it at the same time.

An admonition I remembered reading on a sign in the national park came to my mind:

> "AGITATED BEARS CAN BE DANGEROUS.
> BACK AWAY SLOWLY, MAKING YOURSELF
> LOOK AS LARGE AS POSSIBLE,
> DO NOT LOSE EYE CONTACT."

Since this didn't seem to fit the present situation, I decided it was time to see if there was any sprinting capacity left in the old legs. I made a quick pirouette to dash to safety, stepped smack-dab into a large mess of fresh bear scat, and fell flat on my face. You know scat – it's the polite term for POOP. In this case, bear poop, which is mighty slippery stuff.

So here I was, prone in the brambles, face down in the sticker bushes, preparing to be eaten alive or at least trampled to death right there in the berry patch, my pitiful remains not to be discovered until the old folks arrived, chattering excitedly about the good old days while carrying their pails and buckets to pick my blackberries. Well, at least it will be a memorable moment for them. Give 'em something new and different to talk about.

It was then that a most remarkable thing happened. From the inner reaches of the thicket, came the unmistakable sound of a guttural voice speaking in a deep, resonate rumble: "Never kick a fresh turd on a hot day."

Now there I was, lying face down in the brambles – prone in a mess of crushed, nearly ripe blackberries, suffering the indignity of having been felled by bear poop and resigned to ending my allotted span alone and unnoticed, but I still managed to recognize those words as one of Harry Truman's favorite sayings. I think it was old Harry's way of saying, "don't disturb the status quo," or "don't do something stupid," or maybe just plain "let sleeping bears lie."

The latter seemed most appropriate for the occasion, but the question of greater importance was "who" or "what" was quoting old "Give 'em Hell" Harry up here in this primitive wilderness. I was hoping that perhaps I was the butt of somebody's warped sense of humor, but based on the sound of that strange voice and the

7

unmistakable bear snuffle which preceded it, such was not the case.

In the present circumstances, I felt it was time for me to "reevaluate my position," which is the modern American way of saying "what the hell do I do now?"

Frankly, I hadn't the foggiest idea. All I could think of at the time was a quotation from a desperate situation of a different sort:

"Houston, we've got a problem."

It was feeble, but it was the best I could do.

Pondering a course of action in a desperate situation.

CHAPTER TWO

A Bear of a Different Color

It hardly needs to be said that a lot of things were racing around in my brain as I lay face down in that remote blackberry patch, probably bleeding, my pulses running totally out of control, certain that a black bear was somewhere very close by. Not just a run-of-the-mill black bear, but one who speaks English.

That's not the whole of it either. The creature recites quotations – Harry Truman, no less. I must have stunned myself in the fall, I thought, yet just out of sight I could still hear that snuffling sound along with heavy, bear-like breathing, and a slobbering noise that sounded like a bear eating blackberries. Stunned or not then, there was a bear over there and I had a feeling that he was watching me, though I couldn't see him. Or was it her?

The thought flashed through my mind that I should worry about the sex of the beast later. Right now the more pressing matter was to determine a course of action.

I recalled psychology lessons I

This is Ralph before he got his fur coat. He was celebrating his first Independence Day.

used to teach about the power of adrenaline and the "fight or flight" reaction as it affects primitive man (and beast). In my present predicament the adrenaline would take care of itself, since I could hear it roaring in my ears like ocean surf in a winter storm. And it seemed to me that the choice between fight and flight was an easy one. There's no way I'm going to fight a bear, I said to myself, not even if he's an old toothless one who has just had his toenails clipped. Not even a bear who speaks English. I was left, then, with the "flight" option and here, of course, I use the word as a derivative of the verb "to flee," although true flight would have been the much preferred means of exit.

Fleeing takes several forms: high speed, medium fast, slow, and nonchalant saunter. For all I knew, it might be possible to sneak away from a bear so slowly that he wouldn't even know you had escaped, but this didn't seem likely, especially from one who was smart enough to speak English. I have read that bears, though they prefer to "lumber," can actually run very fast for short distances. Up to 40 mph, they say.

Since I can't actually run fast for even forty feet, option number one was easily put aside. The medium fast and slow options seemed kind of wishy-washy. A trot or a fast walk, maybe? Either one seemed like a sure invitation to be eaten by the bear, if such was his intent. My research on bear behavior shows that they despise cowardice and dislike having people walk or run away from them without excusing themselves first.

So, then, my course was clear. My only hope was subterfuge, a course of action so clever that the brute would not realize he was being hoodwinked.

Here's how I'll work it, I thought to myself: calmly stand up, brush myself off, pick the stickers out of my clothes, put my hands in my pockets, whistle a happy tune and saunter off. As soon as I'm out of sight, I'll run like hell.

Good plan. Poor execution.

First off, my legs wouldn't function properly as my knees kept buckling. My whistling pucker wouldn't work and I couldn't see very well, making it hard to find the trail. All is lost, I thought. I must make my peace with the world, accept the inevitable and let the bear have his way with me. At that moment, when all seemed lost, I distinctly heard what sounded like a chuckle behind me and in that same rumbling voice came the words, "Relax, old man, I'm not going to eat you. For the most part I'm a vegetarian."

"Okay, okay, now I get it," I thought. "I'm the victim of a practical joke. It's one of those old dudes from over at the development doing a Halloween-type prank, trying to scare me out of 'his' berry patch." Now my dander was up a little, and my terror adrenaline was quickly replaced by my pissed-off adrenaline.

"I'll bet it's that Elbert jerk I had the argument with last year," I said to myself. "I'll show him he can't intimidate me with his childish practical jokes."

Nevertheless, I was beginning to feel just a tad foolish. There's no telling what mischief an overactive imagination will conjure up.

"Talking bear, indeed," I thought. "Let this little episode be a lesson to you."

I decided to go around the bend in the trail and tell the old geezer that I wasn't fooled for a second by his juvenile antics. So around the bend I went and a little bit farther, and there, not more than fourteen feet away, sitting on a stump with his legs crossed, was a large black bear. He was eating berries out of his hand and making slobbering noises. Every once in a while he curled his lip up like maybe he'd gotten a sour one. My mind was so focused on the idea that it was Elbert over there playing a joke on me that my first thought was that this bear had eaten him, which shows how your mind can play tricks. I had just shifted mental gears from bears to practical jokers and was having trouble shifting back. But there was no question about it, this was a real bear.

"Uh, ah, I'm sorry," I stammered. "I thought you were somebody else." I began what I thought was a graceful retreat, backwards. "I'll be running along. I just remembered something I need to do down at the house."

In a voice that sounded just a little bit more like an order than an invitation, the bear spoke in his curious rumbling mumble, "I don't want to seem impolite, but now that you're finally here, why don't you just sit down and stay awhile. There are things I'd like to talk to you about. Just come over here and take my stump, I'll sit on the ground."

Talking bear indeed.

With that he rose from his seat, lumbered a short distance and settled himself, bear-like, on the ground, unmindful of the thorns and brambles. Now when a bear sits down, he suddenly seems more comical than threatening, and my curiosity about his sex was quickly answered, too. This was a man bear. Comical male black bear or not, I quickly noticed that he had positioned himself between me and the exit from the berry patch. My path to safety was blocked. He saw my discomfort.

"It's plain to see that you're ill at ease," he mumbled. "Please, let's have no fidgeting. I want you to relax and take it easy." He fixed me with a penetrating gaze, but it was all I could do to maintain eye contact.

"It's understandable that you're nervous, what with all the misinformation spread around about how we bears are unpredictable and dangerous. Some are, I'm usually not. First, I want to tell you I've been watching you puttering around your shop down there, and, parenthetically, if you don't mind me saying so, there is more puttering than productive activity. Nevertheless, it occurs to me that you seem to be a trustworthy sort and I assure you that I'm no threat to you as long you behave yourself."

I wasn't at all sure what I had heard. Did he use the word "parenthetically" or was it my imagination? "I'm sorry," I said. "Would you mind repeating what you just said?"

"Yes, I would," he mumbled very slowly. "What I said was, you don't work very hard and I think maybe you can be trusted and perhaps I won't eat you. I really don't like the taste of people."

This time I clearly understood what he said and I liked the part about being trustworthy. I'm a sucker for this kind of flattery. I began to feel better. Imagine being thought of as trustworthy by a bear, especially one that uses big words like "parenthetically." It boggles the mind.

To this day, I'm still flabbergasted when I think about it, but for the next hour-and-a-half that bear and I had a most pleasant and wide-ranging conversation in the middle of that blackberry patch.

We exchanged personal biographies, opinions on politics and economics, and what we both agreed was the rather sorry state of society in general. I learned that we shared many views in common.

And before the time was gone, I even got so I could understand his peculiar manner of speaking. His mumble had a singular melodious timbre, sort of a rumbling basso-profundo which was unique and totally suited to his character.

As I arose to leave, I remembered that I was supposed to be afraid of this creature and realized with amazement that I was not.

We agreed to meet again the next day to continue our discussion. I left our little meeting place in a strangely euphoric state of mind. It seemed as though I had accomplished something quite remarkable, and I suppose having an intellectual conversation with a black bear did come under that heading. It was a circumstance that was going to take some getting used to.

As I started back toward the exit, he fixed me with his beady little eyes. "Now don't go blabbing all over the neighborhood about our meeting here. The last thing I need is a bunch of damned tourists and TV people running all over the place."

"Are you kidding?" I laughed. "Most of the people around here think I'm crazy already. If I told them I've been talking to a bear it would just confirm their suspicions."

As I rounded the bend heading out of the thicket, I heard his final comment, "And scrape that shit off your shoe. You don't want to track it into your house." This is the kind of straightforward talk I like. I whistled a little tune and set off down the trail.

And in a small patch of grass, I scraped the "bear nutrients" off my shoe.

CHAPTER THREE
We Strike a Bargain

I don't think I slept much that night and as I gradually came awake I began to review what I believed to have been an interesting dream – one of those vivid kinds of dreams that happen just before you wake up. This one was all about a bear, a talking bear, and it wasn't more than a second or two before the realization dawned that this had not been a dream. I had indeed spent part of the previous day in the company of an erudite black bear discussing the affairs of the world – both his world and mine.

Usually the most exciting thing that happens hereabouts is when the neighbors start threatening each other with legal action over two or three inches of real estate. To the best of my knowledge, bears have never been much of a topic of conversation around here, except for the ones I occasionally carved out of wood to sell to the passing tourists. Shoot, I didn't even know we had real bears in the neighborhood, let alone an English-speaking one practically in my back yard. Try to imagine such a thing happening to you.

Anyway, I was eager to get back up to the bear's lair to continue our discussion, although I was not eager to climb that beastly hill. The day promised to be a hot one. Under different circumstances I wouldn't have even considered going up there, but my head was buzzing with a thousand bear questions. To get the answers I must make the climb, like it or not.

As I passed by my shop, I was reminded that I hadn't decided what to make out of that log. It was still lying there, a silent reminder that I wasn't getting any work done.

"Got more important things to do right now," I said to the log. "I'll get around to you later."

As expected, there was no reply but I think a germ of an idea was born as I set out for the dreaded hill climb.

The scramble to the top was no easier than it had been the day before, and on the way up I thought how nice it would be to have an inclined railway so I could just push a button and ride up; much too expensive, of course, but interesting to think about. I sat down to rest part-way up. I let my imagination take over and had a little conversation with myself.

"How about this," I said. "I put the bear in a cage, advertise him as the world's only talking bear, charge a stiff admission fee and make enough money to build an electric tramway to the top and a whole lot more. We would have little programs up there and let the bear read poetry or something. Or maybe just answer questions about bear things."

Remember what I said earlier about talking to myself? It's nonproductive and seldom breaks new creative ground. I can just imagine what that bear would have to say about my plan to put him in a cage. He didn't especially strike me as a poetry-type either, and furthermore, I would soon be overrun by hordes of angry, long-haired animal rights people carrying signs, screaming into bullhorns and carrying buckets of cow blood to throw on my customers. Not to mention all the Fish and Wildlife people with their dart guns, radio collars and clipboards. To hell with the inclined railway – it's not worth it. I'll just build a trail to the top.

Eventually I got up there, accompanied by the usual gasping and heavy breathing and with a couple more rest stops along the way. Assuming that I would find my new friend in the same place as he was yesterday I headed for the berry patch. I didn't want to startle him by arriving unannounced, so I began a little whistle and did some rather loud banging about. I've always heard that bears dislike abrupt interruptions to their daily routine. As I arrived at the entryway to the thicket I sang out in a rather quiet way, "Hey, Bear, are you here?"

Back came the now familiar rumbling mumble. "Yeah, right here. Same place. Come on in."

Sure enough, there he was. Sitting on the same stump, legs crossed, eating berries, smacking his lips and slobbering. I noticed that he had apparently dragged a large chunk of log out of the underbrush to serve as a seat for me. He pointed at it with a large handful of fearsome looking claws and invited me to sit.

"It's a good thing you're not trying to sneak up on somebody," he said. "A locomotive could climb that hill with less confusion. A bit out of shape, are we?" he asked sardonically.

I had a cutting rejoinder on the tip of my tongue, but withheld it on the premise that it might be imprudent to display my usual flair for sarcasm so early in our friendship. Actually, I was so out-of-breath from the climb I would have had little

A noisy bear is a dead bear, my friend.

success in a shouting match anyway. Instead, I quietly offered that I was getting on in years and hadn't been doing much climbing since I was so busy in my shop, etc., etc.

The bear smiled knowingly. "Of course," he said. "I understand. But if you're going to hang around with me, you'll need to have some lessons in stealth. I remember my mother telling us kids that a noisy bear is a dead bear. As usual my twin brother Romeo wasn't listening and he's dead now, carried off by a bullet shot from close range. 'Dumb Romeo' we used to call him. He seldom listened to advice from anyone."

"A pity," I said. "By the way, do you have a name you go by? It's inconvenient just calling you 'Bear.' Might even be insulting, for all I know."

"Raaupf," he snorted. I waited politely, thinking he was clearing his throat.

"Raaupf, dammit. Raauph. My mother named me RAAUPF."

"I'm sorry," I said lamely. "Maybe we can get something for that throat. I've got some stuff down at the house that might help."

"Oh, shut the hell up," he said with some heat. "I'm trying to tell you my name and I'm only going to do it once more. My name is Raaupf."

Maybe some trial and error would help, I thought. "Rolf?"
"No."
"Raul?"
"No."
"Roof. Alf. Olaf?"
"No, no, no."
"Ralph?"
"By George, I think he's got it," the bear growled with some

relief. Most of the conversations we had in the early days of our acquaintanceship went on very much like that – tedious and difficult. Gradually we learned from each other, groping and fumbling along.

I asked if he had another name and he was clearly reluctant to tell me. After a lot of backing and filling, he confided that his middle name was "Beauregard."

"God knows where she came up with it," he said. "I guess it's French or something. Beauregard, can you believe that? Talk about your mouthful."

"Actually, Beauregard is a French name," I volunteered, hoping to impress the bear with my worldly knowledge. "It means 'beautiful to look at.' Your mother must have thought you were something special."

"Hell," the bear said with disgust. "When the old bag kicked me out of the den, she hollered that I was **TOO MUCH TO BEAR!** For

a long time I actually thought that my name was 'Tumuchtu Bear.' Get it? Very funny. My brothers used to call me 'Muchtu.' They did until I kicked their little butts, that is."

For the most part, our conversation went on in a like manner for an hour or so as we cautiously tried to feel each other out. I began to get the impression that my new friend had been starved for somebody to talk to for so long that he was just warming up. I had the feeling that he might go on talking non-stop

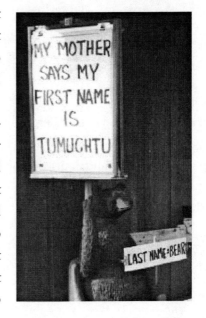

until sundown. By now I had eaten so many not-quite-ripe blackberries that I was beginning to feel some discomfort. The sun was becoming unbearably hot.

"How about we ease ourselves over in the shade someplace?" I suggested.

"Good idea," said Ralph. "But we, I mean I, mustn't show myself. You have no idea how many hazards there are around here. Bears like me are fair game for every redneck with a gun and every dog looking for excitement. Constant vigilance is the price of liberty, you know. Life *and* liberty," he added.

We found ourselves a convenient spot, still concealed, but in deep shade. Ralph lumbered over, rolled himself in the grass several times and then flopped down against a small tree in his familiar comical attitude, but this time with his hind feet flat together and front paws spread out at his sides. He braced himself and rubbed his back vigorously against the tree trunk.

"That rolling around stirs up the ticks some. Keeps them on their toes. Don't want them to think they're getting a free ride all the time."

At the mention of ticks I may have instinctively shifted my position a bit, then immediately regretted it. I still didn't know how easy it might be to offend this creature.

"Don't worry about the ticks," he said. "Those bugs would much rather be on me than on you. They're the bane of a bear's life – next to dogs and rednecks with guns, that is."

"So," I asked, changing the subject. "You have kinfolk in the area?"

"There may be a few left around here, but I hardly ever see any of them. I've had several brothers and a couple of sisters that I know of. They scatter all over the place. I've heard that one of them is now a floor ornament in a cabin over near Coon Lake; had a cousin who ended up in the stew down in McCleary during the Bear Festival. It's getting damn hard just to stay alive anymore. Hardly ever see my mother since she kicked me out of the den when I was two years old. To paraphrase a little green amphibian I know, 'It ain't easy being a bear.' I still go out looking for my kind during the rutting season, but they're getting harder to find. It's a damn shame what's happening to us bears. The government spends millions of dollars on owls and beetles and weeds and not one damn red cent to keep the black bear from being harassed, hounded, badgered and exterminated."

The bear peered at me intently. "You got any influence in Olympia? Get some laws passed, maybe?"

"I'm afraid not, friend," I replied. "I'm not politically active. In fact, I'm definitely what you would call politically inactive. I much prefer griping about the system from the sidelines. One can be more objective that way."

"Those are close to my sentiments, too," the bear agreed. "But I want to tell you there was a time when I was young and idealistic and thought I could save the world for bears through the legislative process. Even wrote a Bill of Ursine Rights that was adopted as part of the OWL Party platform. You remember the OWL Party,

I much prefer griping about the system from the sidelines ...

21

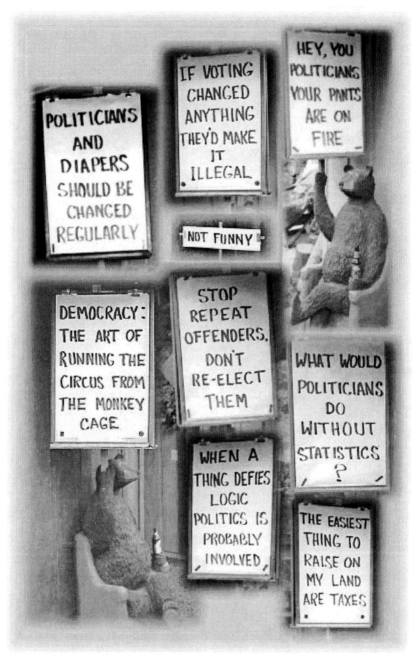

One of Ralph's favorite topics is politics and politicians. I always had the feeling that he would have gone into politics if he could have. He was born to talk and had an opinion on every subject.

don't you? OWL stands for 'Out With Logic.' Anyway, the OWLs weren't taken too seriously and they faded away. Naturally my second amendment referred to the right of bears to arm themselves but this sort of levity gets you nowhere with politicians. Self-importance is the politician's birthright; that, and the propensity to blather. Did you know that we have a state insect? Why not a state bear, then, with full protection of the law?"

"By the way," said the bear, fixing me with a penetrating look. "Are you aware that it is illegal for a human like you to have unlawful contact with a wild animal like me?"

"Who says?" I inquired with surprise.

"Your busybody legislature says!" replied Ralph. "It's illegal to have unlawful contact and that's typical redundant legislative blather, not to mention stupid."

The bear was getting himself all worked up, pacing back and forth, waving his arms. Apparently politics was something that stirred his deepest emotions and I began to fear for my safety. He brought his face close to mine, spraying me with bear spittle. I was nearly overcome with bad bear breath. He was so close that I watched a flea walk slowly across his nose.

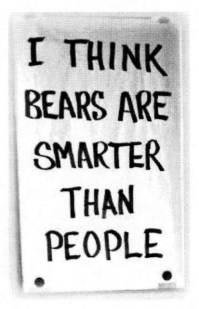

"Bears are absolutely smarter than people," he snorted, "and nothing's so bad that politicians can't make it worse. They're nothing but a bunch of busybody tinkerers. I bet I'm breaking some law just by sitting here."

I was caught with my back against the tree with no avenue of escape. I'm a goner, I thought. An excited bear is unpredictable. I've read it in the books. His beady little eyes were bright, his pupils dilated.

"Oh, I couldn't agree more," I stammered. "You're absolutely right, no question about it." I thought it was by far the best course of action to agree with everything he said. I couldn't be sure whether his heated oratory would convert itself into some kind of physical threat to me or not.

"And do you know if voting changed anything, they'd make it illegal," he said somewhat more calmly.

I agreed again.

"Sorry I got all excited there. Politics does that to me. I'm just afraid that this country is headed for the dumpster and I'm concerned about the fate of *your* species as well as mine. Mostly mine. Politics is the art of running the zoo from the monkey cage. You've heard that expression before, haven't you?"

"Oh, sure, I've heard it," I said.

"I made it up," he said with that lopsided little grin that he showed occasionally. It was a trait I had noticed previously and one he used when he wanted to confuse you about whether he was telling the truth or not.

"I've decided that my main mission in later life is to spread confusion. It's my strong belief that it's better to be confused than to go around thinking you know what's going on. Everybody lies; doesn't matter, nobody's listening. You get my drift?"

His logic was unassailable, I think, but he sure had *me* confused. Somehow it seemed like we had lost our focus. Perhaps it would be best to change the subject.

"Mind if I ask you a question?" I asked.

"Fire away," he mumbled. "I haven't had anybody to talk to for a long time and I've got opinions on any subject you can come up with. Try me."

"You seem unusually well read for a bear. How do you come by all the smarts? I mean, most bears can't even talk let alone use big words."

"Oh, most bears can talk all right, they just don't choose to talk to *people*. Most everything I know I learned at my mother's knee. When we were little, Mother read to us every night at beddy-bye. First it was Dick and Jane, then Peter Rabbit. Winnie the Pooh was my favorite; lots of subtle humor there. I wanted to grow up to be just like Pooh until I found out his head was full of sawdust. No wonder he had a very small brain. As I got older I discovered that bears with very small brains don't last long in the real world. Would you believe that when I was a cub I read just about everything William Shakespeare ever wrote?"

"No, I probably wouldn't believe that." I said with some misgivings, not being too sure how safe it was to question his veracity. "How'd you come by the Shakespeare stuff?"

"The way I heard the story was that my great-grandmother Gertrude - she was the Queen of Denmark, you know - found an almost complete set of Shakespeare in a garbage can down near Victor. It was one of those cheap sets, you know, the kind they used to give away when you joined a book club. Most of the stuff was there, except *King Lear* and *Henry the Fifth* had some kind of spaghetti sauce spilled all over them and they were too hard to read."

"Your great-grandmother was the Queen of Denmark?" I asked incredulously, thinking it best to carefully humor this creature until I could make a graceful exit. It was becoming fairly clear that I was dealing with a nut case. The thought flashed through my mind that this wasn't a particularly surprising turn of events. A talking bear was already straining credulity to its limits and a sane talking bear seemed like too much to expect.

Ralph regarded me with just the slightest hint of disgust. "I see we have some education to do here, but I suppose it's not unexpected," he said slowly. "Now listen carefully. Granny was not the Queen of Denmark. She just took the name of Gertrude, who was the Queen of Denmark. Hamlet's mother. You know, in Shakespeare's play. Now, mind you, I don't remember my great-grandmother, but I used to hear stories about her; how she went around smiting her brow and crying things like 'Out damned spot, out, I say' and 'No, no, the drink, oh my dear Hamlet, I am poisoned." Ralph was waving his arms around to suit the dialogue, clearly caught up in the emotions of the scene.

"Granny actually wanted to start a troupe of Shakespearean bears, except back then it would have been hard to get enough bears together to pull it off. She had to settle for readings. Everybody in the whole damned extended family had to read Shakespeare, even things like *Cymbeline* and *Timon of Athens*."

Ralph had fixed me with a kind of beady-eyed intensity. "You don't believe a damn bit of this, do you?"

I decided to take the bull by the horns. I would find out how sensitive this creature was.

"Actually," I said with some trepidation, "I don't. My usually very open mind is about to go shut. With all due respect, it all sounds like a lot of hogwash. My credulity is severely strained, but what the hell, tell me more."

Ralph appeared to be totally unaffected by my skepticism. "Believe as you will, my friend, but in any case it would probably be 'bearwash,' not hogwash. Feel free to question me on any aspect of Shakespeare that strikes your fancy. Quiz me."

"My knowledge of Shakespeare," I said, suddenly being reminded of a long forgotten episode in my early years, "is limited to the time I read the part of Julius Caesar when he was stabbed by Brutus on the steps of the Forum or wherever the hell he was. I was in high school and for some unknown reason everybody had to read Julius Caesar. I thought this was a defining moment in my secondary education and I could hardly contain myself as we came to the dramatic moment when Caesar cries 'et tu Brute' and falls dead. The only problem was that since I was also studying French at the same time I pronounced 'et' as 'ay,' as one would in French, and 'Fisheyes Cochran,' the bane of every

I see we have some educating to do here.

English student in the school, turned her withering gaze on me and corrected my faulty pronunciation.

"That is et. Et. The Latin, please."

I think my career in dramatics and probably my interest in Shakespeare both ended then and there. Ah, 'tis strange what minor memories will stay with a man who has a span of sixty years to choose from. I waited for a reaction from my companion. Ralph had a puzzled expression.

"Your story touches me, but I can't place your last quotation. From *Henry the Second*, perhaps?"

"I just made it up," I said with a very small smirk.

The bear sighed resignedly. "Never mind, I'm getting a bit rusty on the whole thing, anyway. One's interests change. Survival has supplanted Shakespeare. Just staying alive is where it's at now. All the books are still in Mother's cave. Pretty dog-eared, but still mostly legible. You know our whole family got a lot of ridicule about our reading habits. That ruffian bunch over at Toonerville a long time ago named us the 'Shakesbears.' I guess the name stuck. So to answer the question you asked me a long time back, my full name is Ralph Beauregard Shakesbear. I think."

We could hear a dog barking in the distance; Ralph's attitude changed from reflection to studied alertness. "That's the old hound named Hornblower. He's a long way off. We're in no danger. He's supposed to be one of those coon dogs, but he's scared to death of bears. He's probably treed a cat. Makes him feel important."

He scuffed the dirt with his foot. Several ants scurried off in alarm.

"I don't want you to get the idea that I'm some kind of intellectual snob just because I know Shakespeare. I'm a bear who can hold his own with any of 'em. My reading tastes are quite eclectic. I've even read the Bluejackets Manual. Cover to cover."

"Where in hell did you get a copy of the Bluejackets Manual?" I asked.

"Garbage can. Same place I get most everything," he said.

"I've read most all of Louie Lamour's stuff. Lots of those cheap romance novels. You can find all kinds of those in the garbage. I even read that little story you wrote about your statues down there on the road. That *'Waiting For The Stage'* thing. Would have been a better yarn if you had put some bears in it."

"How did you get hold of that?" I asked with surprise.

"You left your shop unlocked one night so I just walked in and took it. You need to be more careful or somebody will clean you out. Lots of expensive stuff in there." The bear rolled over on his back and scratched his belly.

"What else do you want to know about me?" asked the bear, who seemed to be mellowing.

"Where do you live? I inquired. "You got a den somewhere? A cave, maybe?"

The bear gazed into the distance, and there was a long pause before he spoke.

"That's the one question I can't answer. Even though I know you're a trustworthy fellow and would honor an oath of secrecy, I dare not tell even you. If somehow the word got out about where I live, my life wouldn't be worth a plug nickel. Is it 'plug' nickel or 'plugged' nickel? Never have figured it out!"

"Anyway, all I can tell you is that I have two residences; one for day, one for night. So far they are very secure, but I never stop looking over my shoulder. As I've already said, it's not an easy life. The biggest problem is the dogs. There's getting to be dogs all over

29

the place up here. Civilization is closing in on me. And while I'm on that subject, just why in hell do they call it civilization? There's precious little that's civil about it. It's like saying you can have a civil war. You people have a very strange language..."

I was suddenly afraid that the bear was off on another filibuster and I determined to cut it off. "Tell me about the dogs, Ralph. You mentioned dogs being a problem."

If it were possible for a bear to get red in the face I'm sure this is the point at which it would have happened. The bear stood up on his hind legs and struck a fighting pose. My God, I thought, this

creature is bigger than I thought. He reminded me somehow of John Wayne about to take on a saloon full of ugly bad guys.

"These dogs around here are mostly cowards. They've learned from experience that in packs of less than four I'll whup 'em every time. Trouble is they keep barking and howling until they get reinforcements or until they attract one of those damned rednecks with a gun. Things get kinda sticky then, so then I have to go into that 40 mph run that you've read about. That gets rid of the rednecks as long as they're on foot, and assuming that I can dodge the bullets, I've still got the dogs to cope with. The best thing to do is get them all strung out and then pick 'em off one by one."

Ralph made several vicious swipes with his paws to illustrate. He was growling and flailing about in all directions. This was the first time I had heard the bear growl. Instinctively I ducked my head and cringed. Ralph went on with somewhat less passion.

"So far this system has worked pretty well. I've put away my fair share of dogs and they don't bother me too much anymore unless they're having a convention or something over there in that new housing development. Luckily dogs are too stupid to do anything in an orderly way. They're dumber than Winnie the Pooh and they don't have the excuse of having sawdust for brains. There's one long-legged son-of-a-bitch over there calls himself 'Big Red.' Thinks he's my match. Someday we'll have a showdown, I suppose, but I'm getting tired of these games. You know how it is. There's always some hotshot around who thinks he's tougher than the big dude. Goes with the territory, I guess."

Wearily the bear sat back down in the grass. His expression prompted me to ask another question.

"How old are you, Ralphie?"

As soon as the word was out of my mouth I regretted it. This bear was not a "Ralphie" type. I held my breath, waiting for an angry reaction. I don't know what possessed me since the only Ralphie I ever knew was a skinny little kid I played with when I was a small boy. There was no reaction and I figured he hadn't heard me. Maybe he suffered fools gladly. I felt like I had dodged a back-hand from an angry bear.

"I don't think I know," he replied. "Maybe ten or twelve years. We don't keep much track of that kind of thing. I've still got some vigor left, though. I still enjoy the companionship of the opposite sex if that means anything. A little fondle and grope now and then gets my blood to running pretty good. Is that a good sign?"

"If memory serves correctly, I think it is," I said, making a little joke. "Say, how long do bears live, anyway?"

"Damned if I know," he replied. "I haven't died yet."

He made a sound which I took to be a laugh.

"Can't tell you, but last time I saw old Mom she had some gray hairs on her muzzle. That probably means she's getting old, right?"

"Probably so," I agreed.

The bear got to his feet. "I think we better adjourn this meeting for today. I have a feeling the old folks from across the way are going to be over here soon to check on the berries. I sure don't want them to see me. That would be a disaster." Ralph shook himself vigorously. Dust, stickers, leaves and dirt flew in all directions. Probably a few ticks, too, I thought to myself.

"What are you going to make out of the new log?" he asked.

"That's exactly what I was trying to decide the other day when I came up here to check out the berries and ran into you instead," I said. "I still haven't decided."

"How about a statue of me?" He struck a comical pose, wearing what I took to be a silly grin.

"Might be a good idea," I mused. "I'm pretty good at bears, I've made a lot of them."

"Yeah, I know. I remember that grizzly you made. I was glad you sold that big bugger. I don't like grizzlies even when they're made out of wood," he said with feeling. "I know there's no grizzlies around here, but Mother used to tell us about them when we were little cubs. Said that the grizzly would get us if we didn't eat our porridge. Grizzlies eat black bears, ya know."

"What kind of a pose would you like?" I asked.

"How about a Napoleon - hand inside the coat, heroic expression?" He struck the pose.

"No good," I said. "Makes you look like you've got a bellyache."

"George Washington maybe? Finger up in the air, making profound pronouncements? Like this."

"Won't do," I said. "My log isn't long enough. Anyway it makes you look like you're trying to hail a cab."

Ralph backed up, sat down on a stump and crossed his legs, thinking.

"Hey, that's it! Perfect!" I said. "Just the way you were when I first saw you. Gives you kind of a dignified look. Now here's another idea. Suppose we have your hand up in the air and I'll fix it so you can hold a sign. Then if there's some kind of comment you want to make, you just give it to me and I'll write it up for you."

"Okay," said the bear. "Sounds good to me. I've got plenty of things I want to tell you *Homo sapiens*. Maybe I can wake you up. It's about time we bears were heard from. How's this for a start?"

THE HELL WITH THE OWLS. SAVE THE BEARS.

I smiled at the idea. But if I had given the concept sufficient

Ralph could hardly wait to get his propaganda campaign started.

thought at the time, I surely would have made other arrangements. As it was, I innocently walked right into a bear trap, although it was to be quite awhile before I felt the tightening of the noose. At the moment I was simply pleased that I had found a subject for a carving in that cedar log that had been troubling me for so long. A bear holding a sign of clever comments. How quaint, I thought. Little did I know.

"How's about I bring the camera up the next time I come and I'll take some pictures from different angles. Makes it easier to do the carving."

"Good. But don't come until I let you know the coast is clear."

"How am I going to know that?" I asked.

"Easy," he said. "You know that big stump halfway down the hill? Really big fir tree? You can see it from your house. It's got a crack through the middle of it. When you see a stick with a little rag tied to it stuck in that crack, that means it's okay to come up. Got that?"

"Oh, boy," I said eagerly, doing my best to imitate an excited small boy. "Just like the clubhouse stuff we did when we were kids! Can we build a camp, too, Bear? Huh, huh? Can we, Ralph?"

My attempt at juvenile excitement was not good.

"Never mind the bad humor. You just watch for the signal. If you come up here any other time you won't find me around. And listen, if it's a hot day the next time you come, how about bringing a six-pack? All this talking makes me mighty thirsty. Be sure they're longnecks though, I can't drink out of a can, you know."

"Right," I said as I started down the trail. "I'll bring a can of flea powder, too."

"Very funny," he growled. "Now get out of here before I change my mind about that vegetarian diet. By the way, I prefer the name Ralph. Ralphie is a name you use for skinny little kids and wimpy bears."

Without doubt, along with everything else, that damned old bear could read my mind.

The old devil could read my mind, too.

CHAPTER FOUR
We Make a Deal

The next time I went up the hill I took the camera and a couple of six-packs of longneck Buds, and the bear and I had a long session of posing and filming. Now for a creature who had somehow managed to master the English language and who had a remarkable grasp of both basic and arcane knowledge, this bear was just plain dumb about some things. He actually thought it "hurt" to have your picture taken and it took almost an hour of earnest cajolery to disabuse him of the notion. By that time he'd consumed all but two of those beers and didn't seem to care if it would hurt or not.

I finally shot up a good part of a roll of film and thought I had captured him in the pose I wanted. As a matter of fact, if you get right up close to the wooden replica that sits outside my shop and examine his expression closely, I think you'll agree that I've faithfully captured the expression of a bear who has just consumed 120 ounces of beer. It's a kind of "what me worry?" look of dreamy indifference, which belies his real character.

Before we got through with our session that day the wily old beast tried to talk me into going down that brutal hill to get him another six-pack and it began to dawn on me that maybe I had been "snookered." Could it be that he used that fear of cameras business just to drink up all my beer? I resolved to be on my guard in the future.

It was quite a while before I went back up the hill to talk to my new friend. There was a lot of work that I had to do before I would have time for casual chit-chat, even though I was itching to ask him about a lot of stuff I had thought of since our last conversation. Anyway, I had the right photo to use as reference for my "bear in a chair" carving and the 93-year-old log was ready to go. All I had to do was start. But already I could feel the pangs of procrastination and I realized that if I didn't stifle them promptly the summer would be over, the monsoon season would overtake me, and the job wouldn't get done, disappointing the bear.

I had the feeling that a disappointed bear might be uncooperative and prone to lose interest in the whole project. Damn! If I had known then what I know now, I would not only have encouraged him to lose interest, I would have insisted on it. I would have sent that quotation-spouting, insufferable, self-important creature back to wherever he came from.

Do you all remember the story about the guy who somehow got hold of a tiger by the tail? He wanted to let loose in the worst way, but knew if he did the tiger would surely eat him. Well, I was about to get a bear by the tail and even though this bear assured me that I was his friend, he was still a bear with all the characteristics we associate with beardom.

Think about it, if you can. Would you turn your back on a half-wild bear? Even one you have had close conversational relations with in a berry patch and with whom you had shared alcoholic libations?

Bears change their minds a lot and there is always some suspicion about their mental stability. Nevertheless, I had promised this old devil that I would faithfully record his wit and wisdom on a sign down on the highway for the edification of thousands in the motoring public to enjoy (or get upset about). What was I thinking about?

Now today, after almost ten years of doing just that, his fans have come to expect and depend on this form of cheap entertainment, complaining when the signs aren't changed at regular intervals or when they occasionally become repetitious. Whenever I would politely suggest to the bear that maybe we had worn out the whole concept, he would fix me with that baleful bear stare of his and remind me that we had a deal.

"There's no termination date on our contract, you know," he said once, with just a hint of menace in his voice.

I don't ever remember signing a contract. Good Lord, how long do black bears live anyway?

But I'm getting way ahead of my story.

I decided to put off the actual work of making the bear carving until I built my long-promised switchback trail up the hillside to where the bear hung out. In order to do so I conned my neighbor Wayne into helping me. I told him there was good berry picking up there, but for a whole lot of reasons I didn't mention anything about a talking bear.

Wayne, who had some time on his hands, went right to work breaking ground and roughing out the "right of way" through a maze of obstacles. The only problem was that as he got close to the top he began to lose interest and instead of making the trail in long and easy switchbacks all the way, he got within about fifty feet of the summit and went straight up.

This wouldn't do. The trail was going to be tough enough to negotiate as it was, and to face that last fifty-foot grade in a state of exhaustion could be an unwise test of endurance.

Well, I finally got the thing realigned and then improved it to the point where even an old guy like me could make it to the top without too much of a struggle. It's even an easy passage for a bear, although I made it clear to my friend that I would appreciate it if he would just stay up there in his own territory. He said he had no intention of coming down the hill, but I have a strong suspicion that he does come down sometimes in the middle of the night, just to see what I have written on the sign. He probably wants to make sure that I am transcribing his witticisms faithfully.

By the time that I got all this stuff done, it was getting along toward the end of the outdoor carving season. I'm strictly a fair-weather woodcarver. When the temperature falls, when it rains, or when it even looks like rain (which is most of the time around here), I head inside the shop and stir up the fire. As I remember it, that winter was pretty cold, so I assumed that my ursine friend had probably gone underground somewhere in a state of hibernation and wouldn't be bugging

me about getting his "monument" finished. I was right. I didn't see the old fellow all winter long. This suited me fine.

For some reason I was getting a bit uneasy about this deal I had made. When he had mentioned that we had an open-ended contract of some sort, I wondered if this beast fancied himself to be some kind of a legal expert. I was afraid that maybe he had found law books in a garbage can along with everything else. I resolved to quiz him about this matter if I ever saw him again, doing it in a subtle way that wouldn't make

*... when it even **looks** like rain ... I head inside the shop and stir up the fire.*

him suspect that I took a jaundiced view of the legal profession, no matter whether the lawyers had two legs or four. I was probably worrying about things needlessly, which is a common outcome of huddling around a stove through a long winter conversing with one's self.

When winter reluctantly gave way to spring, I realized that I couldn't put off the project any longer. My conscience wouldn't allow it, so in May of '91 as I remember it, I got out my bear photos, stood that big old log up on one end, made a few preliminary marks to guide my cuts and prepared to go to work.

Let me speak for a minute about the whole process of carving wood with a chainsaw (at least as it happens around here), which may help explain why I find it so easy to procrastinate. After you get the saw ready – sharpened and gassed up – you get into the protective gear: coveralls, ear protection, eye protection, dust mask, gloves. It usually helps to say a few words of encouragement to a chainsaw before pulling the starting rope, especially after the winter layoff. Chainsaws are notoriously temperamental and I think they have a need to feel wanted.

If all goes well, you start the saw and begin to cut. About then, hot breath leaking out around the dust mask condenses on the cool lenses of your spectacles, fogging them up so you can't see what you're doing. This necessitates shutting down the saw to wipe the glasses, which will usually happen several times before the tempera-ture differential is overcome. Once you finally get started, you find that the three cups of coffee you had earlier have begun to create bladder distress. So, the whole starting-up process must be reversed and by now it's nearly lunchtime. Sometimes I wonder how I ever get anything done. Maybe it would be better if I were to start work after *lunch*, rather than after *breakfast*.

I think all this may explain why retired folks are always telling you about how busy they are. They spend most of their time spinning their wheels and slipping their clutches.

In spite of all the obstacles I have outlined above, I got started on the job and, in short order, found myself making good progress. Because the log I was using was barely large enough to contain both the bear and the chair, I had to make the bear smaller than he is in real life. I did manage to get a good-sized potbelly on him however, and captured the dreamy, beer-induced coun-tenance previously mentioned. It wasn't difficult to figure out what to do with the left hand, which is the one not holding the sign. I simply fash-ioned it so as to hold his favorite longnecked beer bottle. This was a nice touch I felt, and one that would please the old reprobate. When not holding a beer it could be used to hold another sign with the punch line on it or maybe just some other object to fit the occasion.

In a week, the job was nearly done. I had caught my friend's true looks and charac-ter from every angle. Oh, no woodcarver is ever completely satisfied with his work for there are the inevitable flaws, but it

Ralph insisted I get the color of his coat exactly right. He also said the long-neck beer bottle would add a "touch of verisimilitude," as he put it.

41

is not the artist's place to point them out. The viewer must discover them for himself, and hopefully he won't.

The final task was to make some kind of a framework to hold signboards that could be reused whenever Ralph came up with something new that he wanted to share with his audience of *Homo sapiens*, as he put it. After much experimentation, I rigged up a contraption that would use cheap newsprint that I could write on with a black felt pen in big enough letters to be readable from some distance down the road in both directions.

I discovered that the maximum number of words that would fit on the sign was about fifteen and they would have to be short words. I knew that this would distress the old blowhard because in fifteen words he is just beginning to get up steam. As a way of introducing

 the sign to the motoring public, I wrote the first message myself. I wrote, **"I'VE GOT SOME IM-PORTANT THINGS TO SAY."**

Several travelers immediately slowed their cars to see what this new attraction was all about. One even backed up and the driver sat there staring, apparently waiting for the bear to say something.

It quickly occurred to me that I *didn't* really have

anything to say, important or otherwise. I had innocently assumed that Ralph would keep me supplied with reams of material as we had sort of agreed to in our last meeting. I was suddenly reminded that our *last meeting* had taken place in the fall and that I hadn't seen or heard from the old beast since.

Bears lead a precarious existence, as Ralph was fond of telling me. Suppose he had become a victim of foul play - "rednecks," dogs, cougars, highway traffic? Why I couldn't even be sure that the old rascal was still alive.

As I stood there viewing my latest creation, my glow of self-congratulation was replaced by a feeling of uneasiness. My gaze strayed up the hill. I had been so preoccupied with finishing my project, that I hadn't watched for our agreed-upon signal. I couldn't see the stump from where I stood, so with some trepidation I climbed the lower part of the trail. There, in the switchback that I call "Big Stump Corner," I saw our secret signal: the stick in the stump with the flag on top! My friend was back! Ralph had returned!

I had no way of knowing how long the signal had been there, but I was certain he would let me know if I had been delinquent in not noticing it sooner. The thrill that I felt in knowing that I had not been abandoned or that my old buddy had not fallen victim to foul play or natural disaster was quickly replaced by a sense of unease. Was I really prepared to

Big stump corner. Half way up the hill Ralph's flag signals that the coast is clear.

face another "season" of coping with this temperamental creature with all of his unreasonable demands, his oversized ego and the strains that he placed upon my time and attention?

I reflected on this problem for about two minutes.

How many people do you know who have an intellectual, half-wild black bear for a friend, I asked myself, and one who speaks fluent English? One who spouts quotations as readily as William Shakespeare and who has such a refreshingly jaundiced view of the human race?

"This is a great opportunity. Grasp it!" I said to myself out loud and I have already told you what this leads to.

"So," I mused. "You will be inconvenienced. Big deal. What else have you got to do with your time? You just might learn something from the old rogue."

Needless to say, I had talked myself into cooperating with the bear although "going to work for him" would be a more accurate way of putting it.

I headed up the trail to see what the old coot had been up to all winter.

CHAPTER FIVE

The Winter Adventures of a Homeless Bear

It had been several months since I had been up the hill and I discovered that the winter weather had made a considerable mess of things. A vicious January ice storm had wrecked the place, and a large madrona tree had fallen right down the middle of the trail. I made a mental note to get around to fixing this problem later on and proceeded with difficulty on a detour around it. I hurried on, anxious to find my bear friend and, as usual, not quite sure why. I couldn't help thinking to myself that my life would be a lot less complicated if I would just forget the beast and mind my own business. And yet, old Ralph Beauregard Shakesbear had sent me the secret signal. He must need me for something, how could I deny him?

"Easy," said the little voice inside me. "And you would, too, if you had a brain."

So, I went trudging onward through the brambles. Onward to an uncertain destiny, feeling noble and martyred. And a little bit stupid.

The rest of the way up the hill was easy. It was still early in the spring and the new growth had not yet taken over the trail the way it would in another month. I found that last year's blackberry patch – the one where I had first made Ralph's acquaintance – was not exactly where it had been a year ago, which is the nature of the wilderness. A berry patch has an uncanny ability to move around from one year to the next based on the availability of water, sunshine, where

45

the seeds land and probably a whole lot of other stuff, too. How should I know? I'll ask the bear about it, he knows everything.

Anyway, it was early in the season so I knew there wouldn't be any other citizens hanging around up there. The bear and I should have uninterrupted privacy, which was a good thing, because we would have a lot to talk about. Now all I had to do was find him.

I didn't think it would be a good idea to shout his name out loud. Even without people around I might attract dogs, which would be just as bad as attracting people. I was pretty sure the old bugger was watching me from somewhere, but how could I tell? How about I just sit down and let him find me, I thought. It was a drizzly day and I wasn't keen on just sitting up there in the damp awaiting his arrival. Who knows when he would show up?

I needn't have worried because hardly five minutes elapsed before I heard the familiar snuffling and slobbering noises and old Ralph lumbered into view. Nothing could have prepared me for his appearance.

This was not the sleek, well-groomed bear that I had last seen in the fall. This one looked 100 pounds lighter - was gaunt and emaciated - and I wasn't at all sure that this was my same old loquacious friend. There was no doubt about his being the right bear, however, when the first words out of his mouth were: "You bring any beer with you?"

He sat down heavily, leaned back against a tree, and sighed wearily. His eyes didn't have their usual sparkle and his breathing was shallow and labored as though he might be suffering from pneumonia. I was almost afraid to ask him what the problem was.

"I have a terrible parch," he mumbled. "I need sustenance."

"No beer," I said. "I had had enough trouble just getting myself up here. Extra weight and I probably wouldn't have made it at all.

"God, you look awful," I ventured. "You been in some kind of trouble?"

"Some kind of trouble doesn't cover the situation. Worst winter of my life. Just one damn thing after another. I'm lucky to be alive."

I guess it was about then that I noticed the scars on the side of his head and the big notch out of his left ear. Clearly he had been in some kind of a scrap. Dogs, maybe; cougars perhaps; but probably another bear I thought, knowing the propensity of the species to quarrel with its own kind. Well, I knew that I would hear the whole story if I would just be patient. As I have said before, this is a bear that loves to talk.

"I heard your chainsaw running down there so I took a chance that you might look up and see the signal in the stump. You got a little time on your hands? I've got to unburden myself. You won't believe what I've been through," Ralph said.

"You're right," I replied. "I probably won't believe it, but I'm willing to give you an hour of my time to hear your story if we can get out of this drizzle. If I sit out here long enough I'll catch my death of something and end up looking as bedraggled as you."

"I know just the place," he said. "It's not far. Come on." He got to his feet with difficulty – sort of like an

It ain't easy being a bear.

old cow getting up – back legs first and then the front legs, one at a time. It was very unbear-like and painful to watch. He began walking slowly in an easterly direction and I followed dutifully behind. I could tell he was in considerable distress, but even so, it occurred to me that the view from the rear of a walking bear has its comical aspects.

A bear has a very loose skin, particularly this one who had lost so much weight, and as he shuffled along in his peculiar pigeon-toed way, with his rear haunches pumping up and down, he had the look of a creature whose hindquarters were propelled by two small boys under a bearskin rug.

Every short while he would stop and peer back at me to see if I was still following, almost like a small child who didn't want to get too far ahead of his mother, lest he get lost. This was totally unlike the self-assured, overly-confident bear I used to know. This guy has had all the stuffing knocked out of him, I thought.

We were entering territory that was totally unfamiliar to me and I was trying to identify landmarks so I could find my way back out, in case I had to do it without my friend as a guide. What if the old boy dropped dead on me out here, I wondered? I doubted that even the Boy Scouts would find me in this jungle. It's amazing how effortlessly an animal the size of a bear can negotiate dense under-brush, leaving no trace of his passing, and do so without a lot of noise and thrashing about. An uncanny skill, I thought. No wonder bears are able to avoid humans so easily.

We trudged on for another five minutes. I followed closely behind my lumbering guide, during which time, for lack of anything else to occupy my mind, I wondered why a bear has a tail. It doesn't serve any purpose or cover anything and it seems like a totally unnecessary appendage.

I was reminded of the time when I carved that big grizzly bear, forgetting to put any tail on him at all, and that guy from California bought the thing at a huge price without realizing that he was being shortchanged. Short-tailed, at least.

Suddenly we entered what I can only describe as the kind of a secret hideout of the sort that would excite the imagination of young readers of those old-time boys' adventure novels. You know, the secret place where only you and your closest chums – the ones who knew the secret password and handshake – were allowed entrance. Just thinking about it made you almost wet your pants with excitement. This was such a place: a tiny clearing surrounded by small hemlock trees acting like a giant umbrella, and protected on all sides by dense underbrush with no visible means of exit or entry. The ground was covered by a thick carpet of needles which were soft and springy and completely dry. Rain could not penetrate the tangled thatch of overhead branches. This was absolute seclusion, away from every vestige of civilization. I felt as though I had found some sort of Shangri-La, yet I knew we couldn't be more than twenty minutes from my home on that busy state highway.

The bear flopped on the ground on his back, totally exhausted, his tongue lolling out of his mouth unattractively. My mental images of secret clubhouses vanished as quickly as they had appeared. What have I gotten myself into, I wondered? I'm out here, lost in some god-forsaken wilderness with a sick bear who may be suffering from malnutrition and who, at any moment, could decide to restore himself by eating me. I began to think I should plan a getaway, even though I had no idea how I would go about it. Then it occurred to me that I could probably distract him from his evil intentions, real or imagined, by engaging him in conversation. It had worked before.

"Well," I said brightly. "So this is where you live. Nice place."

"No," he mumbled. "This is an emergency hideout. I don't live here. God, I feel awful. Damndest bellyache I've ever had."

I saw an opening for a little levity, hoping it might lighten the atmosphere.

"You know what they call a bellyache now?" I asked.

I got no response.

"They call it 'stomach awareness.' It's the latest in political correctness," I said hopefully.

"Shit," was the bear's only comment.

"Any idea what the problem is?" I asked.

"Got into some bad garbage. Real bad garbage."

"Sounds like a redundancy to me," I offered.

"Damn it," he grumbled. "Will you quit with the lousy jokes. Can't you see I'm in distress? You got any Pepto Bismo on you? I think somebody is trying to poison me."

"If you will permit me to say so, I would think that anyone who eats out of garbage cans might expect to get poisoned now and then. Comes with the territory. You never know what people put in there."

"Tell me about it," the bear said wearily. "Would you believe that last winter I ate some of that Viagra. I suppose some guy's wife threw it in the garbage. That came close to killing me, too."

"I didn't know the stuff was poisonous."

"I guess it isn't, but when that farmer over in the valley caught me screwing one of his goats he didn't take it too kindly. I was lucky he was too excited to shoot straight. Missed me with five shots. Set his dogs on me, too, but I outran 'em."

"Sounds like a mighty close call to me," I observed.

"You remember what Winston Churchill said about such

things, don't you?"

I had to confess that I didn't.

"Nothing in life is quite so exhilarating as being shot at without effect. No question the old boy had a way with words. You might save that and put it on your sign down there someday."

Now even under the circumstances of being way out in the woods with a talking bear who was suffering from a monumental bellyache, having the subject of Winston Churchill come up struck me as being singularly bizarre. I tried not to let it show.

I'm beginning to question my own judgement.

"That's too many words for the sign," I said nonchalantly. "It won't fit."

I thought it best to keep the old bugger involved in conversation lest his attention return to his physical discomfort. I would quiz him about Winston Churchill sometime when he was back on his feed or at least when the weather was nicer.

"I notice you've got a notch out of your ear," I said. "You sure that goat farmer didn't nick you after all?"

"I had some other problems, too," he said wearily. "I told you it was a bad winter. I guess I'll have to admit that trouble just seems to follow me around." He roused himself off his back and scratched his foot.

"You know, I'm beginning to question my own judgment. Having 'relations' with a goat in broad daylight in a farmer's back yard shows a singular lack of good sense. Mother told me when I was two years old that I'd probably come to a bad end. I told her that from what I'd heard very few bears die in bed."

"It would help if you were more careful about what you dig out of garbage cans," I said. "At least read the labels on the stuff before you eat it. I've heard that it says right on the Viagra label that the product may cause impaired judgment and unwanted side effects, something like that."

"Yeah, but it doesn't say anything about goats," he observed dryly.

It seemed to me that the bear was beginning to feel somewhat better. The conversation was probably taking his mind off his digestive problems. I had noticed this phenomenon previously. Talking occupied his complete attention. I decided to keep the conversation going.

"Looks to me like you've lost a heap of weight since I saw you last fall. You been sick all winter?"

He was halfway sitting up now in that comical spraddle-legged way with his back against a small tree. He regarded me in a mildly condescending manner.

"You don't know a heck of a lot about bears do you? Hell, I've only been sick since day before yesterday. Bears get real fat in the fall, and then they're supposed to sleep all winter without eating anything. They live off their fat. It's called hibernating. I thought you were smarter than that. Bears don't even get up in the winter to take a leak, did you know that?"

I'm not sure whether I knew it or not, but to one who can't get through a night without a couple of trips to the bathroom, this seemed to be a worthwhile accomplishment.

"So, then, you've been asleep all winter? That's all? Sounds pretty dull to me. Downright boring."

"The fact is, I haven't been sleeping all winter," he said. "Far from it. But I'd probably be a lot better off right now if I had been. Yeah, a whole lot better off."

I could hear the bear's belly rumbling. Then came a loud belch, followed by a fart of robust proportions.

"Jeez, you know where I can find some sassafras? I've got to be more careful about the garbage I eat. Who was it said 'the food here is so bad that when you belch it doesn't remind you of anything?'"

"I think it was some TV comedian, but if you think I'm going to write that on the sign down there, you can forget it. A lot of people around here think that those are my comments on that sign, not yours, and a thing like that could get me in a lot of trouble. I don't do the cooking down there you know."

"I don't watch TV except maybe now and then through somebody's window," rumbled the bear wearily. "Hardly any point in it when you can't hear what's going on."

"Most of the time that would be an improvement," I said.

53

"You know that old guy Ruggles Pester lives down there in that shack by the mosquito swamp? The place with all the old junk cars in the back yard?"

"No."

"Well, he's so damned deaf he keeps his TV going loud enough even the mosquitoes can't stand it. Sometimes I go down there to watch the thing – I can hear it through his walls real easy. He's got a big old dog, but he doesn't bother me because he's gone deaf, too. Doesn't even know I'm there. Trouble is, all the old geezer watches is soap operas and game shows, both of which are guaranteed to soften the brain."

I had to agree with him and went on to suggest that a soft brain was essential to successful television watching. At least, I thought hopefully, we've got his mind off his bellyache. Such was not to be, but he did seem to be perking up some. He sat up a bit and observed me intently.

We must get the attention of the President.

"I want you to write a letter to your President for me."

"Oh, God," I replied without enthusiasm. "Now what?"

"I want you to demand that the government, in the interest of the welfare of the bear population of the United States, undertake a program of inspecting garbage cans for the presence of the E-coli bacteria. Tell him that this would merely be an extension of programs already in place and certainly could

54

be implemented with a minimum of additional expenditures. Demand that, in his upcoming State of the Union address, he announce an initiative – he's big on initiatives, you know – to appropriate, let's say $500 million, to assist this long-ignored segment of our population in overcoming the threat of eating impure garbage with all the health hazards that it presents. Say that this is no less a danger to our national well-being than cigarette smoking, global warming and unprotected sex. You've got to use that kind of bloviated language when you're talking to the government."

"How about a law against putting garbage in garbage cans?" I said sarcastically. "Listen, suppose I go down and find you a Sierra Club type somewhere and send him up here to talk to you. It would be much more effective if you had direct contact with them."

I knew he was getting over his digestive disorder when he practically exploded with indignation.

"Yeah, you idiot! You can do that if you want the whole countryside around here to be declared a bear sanctuary. Those people are crazy. They'll fix it so you won't be able to go in your own house without written permission of the SCBBPP or whatever they call it."

"You remember the spotted owl, don't you? And the snail darter? And the speckled-ass horsefly?"

"Yes and no," I replied without much enthusiasm. "I'm not familiar with that horsefly. By the way, what's that SCBBPP?"

"Stands for something like Sierra Club Black Bear Protection Police or some such. If they find out I live around here they won't rest until they get a collar on me with a radio on it and all that stuff. They've got a fancy word for it, they call it 'instrumentation,' which is just another word for harassment as far as I'm concerned.

They'll probably stick an antenna out my ass. Sometimes they sit up in trees with binoculars, doing studies and writing on clipboards. They'll chase me around with jeeps trying to find out what I'm up to. You know how it goes. The next thing you know you'll have to pay a yearly permit fee for the police to patrol the area and it will be increased each year to pay for additional protection and new police cars. Do you want to hear more? I know a bear this happened to a few years ago. The poor old devil died of exhaustion. Guess what they did then."

"Made stew out of him, maybe," I ventured.

"Hell no. I saw a report of their 'findings' in the paper. 'Cause of death' was listed as starvation brought about by the intrusion of human population on bear habitat. Good joke. Intrusion of busybodies with clipboards would be more accurate. Hell, they chased the old bugger around so he didn't have time to eat. Now, let's get to work on that letter to the President. We've got to tell him about our problem here."

I thought it best that I humor the bear before he got too worked up.

"Okay, Ralph. I'll write the letter for you, but you should know how much good it will do. At best, in about six months we'll get a letter back from some White House functionary which says that the President feels your pain. Hell, he feels everybody's pain. He'll tell you that all that bear pain is caused by insensitive Republicans and that Democrats love bears and your letter, if it ever goes anywhere, will be forwarded to some Deputy Assistant Under Secretary in the Office of the Commissioner in Charge of Bear Problems. End of story."

Actually, I had no intention of writing a letter to anybody. I just said that so he would shut up about his damn garbage problem. I had to make another attempt to change the subject.

"You still haven't told me how you got that notch out of your ear."

"Got that down near Kamilche in November. Visiting an old friend, Loose Bessie. Wanted to see if she was interested in cohibernating with me."

"Seems like a long way to go to seek companionship," I offered.

The bear boosted himself back against the tree until he was sitting up, a sure sign that he was feeling more himself (or getting more excited).

"Dammit," he said. "Companionship in my world is not found on every corner. You people have thinned us out pretty good you know. I've got to go a long way to find my own kind. You have no idea about the challenges involved."

"Here's a 'for instance' for ya: There's probably fifteen highways to cross between here and Kamilche, and any bear that tries to cross a highway has got to be just about tired of living. The first lesson of bear survival is never cross a highway in daylight. Then you've got to get yourself set back in the trees, waiting for a break in the traffic." He struggled to his feet to demonstrate, thought better of it,

MALE BB SEEKS FBB ...
Ralph often advertises for
companionship, "You human
beans have thinned us bears out
pretty good, you know."

57

and collapsed back on his haunches.

"Then you make a run for it. No walking, no trotting. It's a full gallop all the way and a damned crapshoot. Even when you think you've got it made, here comes some macho yahoo halfway across the highway thinkin' he's going to get himself a trophy rug, hollerin' at his old lady, 'watch me pick off this old bugger, Mabel.' Don't get too many chances at a damned bear in this country, anymore, right, Mabel? Get 'em when you can.'"

"Tell me about the notch in the ear, Ralph," I urged. "I'm beginning to take a chill here."

The bear rushed right on. "I'm getting to it, I'm getting to it. Don't rush me."

Clearly his stomach disorder was about to be a thing of the past. One of the more irritating qualities about this old fellow was his insistence on fleshing out his stories with all the details. He always had a beginning, a middle and an end (sort of), with a wealth of self-serving minutia in between. I should have remembered that he became crotchety if he didn't get to do things his way.

"I'm trying to give you a palpable sense of time and place here, so you can feel my pain."

Oh, my God, I thought. What kind of stuff has he been reading now? One of Clinton's speeches, I decided.

"Well, needless to say, I made it across all the highways without being killed and made my way down to Bessie's old haunts, but damned if I could find her. I roamed all around the Kamilche outback where we used to play when I was a cub. Shoot, we used to know every tree, swamp, and trail in the woods. Ah, those were the good old, carefree, halcyon days of youth! Halcyon days, that's a bit from *Henry the Sixth*, Part I, sort of."

The damned old coot was starting to wax poetical again and I was beginning to feel the dampness to an uncomfortable degree.

"Would you believe that right where we had our cub house there's a great big Indian gambling joint?"

"You mean clubhouse, don't you?" and was immediately sorry I had asked.

"Cub house, dammit, where cub bears play. It's a *clubhouse* now. A gambling joint, where you fool human beings are separated from your money. While I was down there I was wondering what would happen if I wandered into the place. I tried to visualize the pandemonium: patrons fleeing for the exits, women screaming, money and poker chips flying. Total chaos. I would swagger in, stand up on my hind legs and claim the property by right of prior ownership. Has a gripping sense of drama, don't you think?"

"Yeah," I said. "I can also visualize Act Two of your gripping drama.
It's the part where there's a large
bearskin full of bullet holes hanging
on the wall with a plaque under it
describing the big Kamilche Bear
Hunt of 1993. I should think that
even a bear who likes to live as
dangerously as you seem to would
know better than to pull a dumb
stunt like that.

"It's an interesting fantasy," I observed. "But we are about to lose
our focus again and if you wish me
to know how you got that chunk

Our old
"cub house" is now
a gambling joint.

out of your ear you had better tell me about it pronto. This drizzle is not letting up. I'm starting to get wet and I have other things to do."

"Stop with your talk about focus, will you," he grunted. "You sound like a damned politician."

"Yeah, a wet politician." I grumbled.

"Alright, here's how it went. I'm roaming around the back woods looking for my old pal Bessie to work out a winter liaison and not having any luck. You have no idea how many little houses and shacks are back in there now. What do all those people do for a living? At night you can see a lot of bright lights going and there are funny smells that are not what you'd call the pristine odors of the forest primeval, if you get my meaning."

"You're in meth and pot territory," I suggested.

"I suppose so," observed Ralph dryly, "and I also know if I knew how to make the stuff, I'd probably go into business myself. Anyway each one of these 'habitations' has a resident tattooed redneck nearby. They all seem to wear camouflaged clothes and everybody has an ugly mud-covered old jeep with tires on it bigger than hot tubs. Some of those people are actually carrying firearms like in the Wild West. 'Packin' heat,' they call it."

"So far you haven't told me anything I don't already know. Have you been up around Toonerville lately?" I asked. Toonerville is another backwoods enclave with a less than savory reputation, but quite a distance away in a different direction.

"That's out of my territory," said the bear. "My second cousin Reginald operates over there and we never got along very well. Always moved in different circles. He's gay, I think. At least he acts like it."

Oh, my God, I thought, what next?

"I didn't know bears were that way," I said casually. I surely didn't want to get into one of those fuzzy arguments about "lifestyles" and all that psychobabble.

"Hell," grumbled the bear. "Everybody has 'em. See that ant running along there?" He pointed at a big, black carpenter ant hurrying across the clearing.

"Ants are gay, did you know that? You watch a hill of ants and you'll see a little bunch of them off by themselves sitting around holding hands. Those are the gay ants. Mostly they just sit around talking. I don't know for sure, but probably about lifestyles and relationships, all that kind of touchy-feely stuff."

I began to understand what my problem was in getting the scoop on the hole in the ear. I had to stop asking questions about Ralph's goofy stories. As long as I kept egging him on we would never get to the end of the conversation. I resolved to just shut up and listen. It might work if I could just do it.

"There's an ant hill around here somewhere," he said, showing an alertness I hadn't seen for a while. "You ever taste ants? They're real good, especially those big carpenter ants that have more meat on 'em. Taste sorta like artichokes."

It was all I could do to avoid a comment, but I knew it would just lead to another open-ended yarn about the eating habits of bears and a long discussion on the relative merits of ants vs. termites as a source of nourishment.

I stood up and brushed myself off.

"I'm heading down the hill," I said. "I've got things to do."

Actually, I wasn't even sure I knew how to get back down the hill, but I wasn't going to let on. Hadn't the foggiest notion, if truth be known, but my ploy worked.

"I thought you wanted to know about the damage to my ear. Sit down and I'll tell you. It's a short story – won't take long. Then I'll show you how to get home."

Damned bear was reading my mind again, too.

"Well, anyway," he said. "I couldn't find any sign of Loose Bessie around Kamilche, but I did hear that she might have gone over to McCleary to visit kinfolk."

Now, if there is anyplace in the whole countryside that a bear with any brains would want to avoid it's got to be McCleary, and the bear looked at me quizzically, obviously expecting me to ask him why in the world he would want to go down there. I kept mum, carrying out my self-imposed gag order. I already knew why a smart bear would want to avoid McCleary, where they shoot bears on sight and make stew out of them.

"You ever hear of the Second Growth and Bear Festival?"

"Yes."

"You know what they do there?"

"Pretty much," I said.

But what I should have said was: yes, I know exactly what they do there. They shoot bears and make stew out of them and I think it's a dreadful shame and a despicable practice and I think we should write the President about it and get Earth First! and the Sierra Club and Friends of the Earth and PAWS mobilized to denounce what they do and have it declared illegal forthwith. Then I should have excused myself, requested that he show me the path home and thereby spare myself another long-winded philosophical discussion about the injustices of the cruel, cruel world he lived in.

I think the bear was sitting in the way of the exit from our little meeting place. I was trapped.

"Sit down," he said in that tone of voice which made it plain that I was to sit down without delay.

"Now I want you to know that McCleary isn't any different than most of the other one-horse towns around here. Years ago the loggers came through and cut down all the big trees and then, of course, all they had left were a lot of little trees. Little trees are a favorite foodstuff of bears, especially in the springtime when the tender bark of the little saplings is very tasty. You give your average bear a choice between the contents of a garbage can or a young fir tree and he'll take the tree every time."

Ralph was on his feet now and I could tell that he was gearing himself up for another one of his lectures. It was too late to head it off.

"Funny thing about your people," he said with growing agitation. "They'll get out their saws and cut down every big tree they can find. Cut 'em up and haul them away and brag about how tough they are. But a hungry bear chews a little bit of bark off a spindly sapling and these same guys go running for their guns, swearing they got to wipe out the bears before they ruin the whole forest."

The bear had now edged up close to me and was getting himself worked up into that oratorical frenzy that I had become all too familiar with. His big snout was so close to my face that I couldn't even focus on the end of his nose. I backed off as best I could, trying to smile agreeably and show interest in his latest tirade on the subject of bear injustice.

Be brave, I thought to myself. This too shall pass.

Ralph rushed breathlessly on while poking me on the chest with a big, evil-looking claw. "You know, I'm convinced that every Podunk community in the country is required to have some kind of civic celebration every year. I think it must be in your Declaration of

Independence, or something. So some years back some genius in McCleary comes up with a big idea on how to fulfill the civic celebration requirement at the same time as solving what they considered their biggest local problem, which is what bears are doing to little bitty second–growth trees. Get all the problems solved in one shot, as it were. So here's what they do: they go out and shoot every damn bear they can get their sights on, boil 'em up in a big pot with a bunch of potatoes, carrots, onions and stuff and call it 'World Famous Bear Stew.' Then they advertise a big one-day whoop-de-do celebration called the 'McCleary Second Growth and Bear Festival,' invite all the rubes from the surround-

ing countryside to come in and watch a one-horse parade with a fire truck and a hay wagon, sell 'em a bunch of trinkets and buckets of World Famous Bear Stew."

Ralph was really warming to his subject.

"They've even got the temerity to advertise this function as McCleary's answer to the loss of our precious forests. There's never any mention of what's happening to the bear popula-tion or who it was cut all the trees down in the first place. My cousin Renaldo who lives down near Brady said he heard that last year they weren't able to ambush enough bears so they extended the stew with an old horse. Said they should have called it the 'Second Growth and Horse Festival.'

Renaldo has a way with words even though he's not very smart."

Ralph concluded his impassioned dissertation with a final re-joinder. "One of these days they're going to cut down all their second-growth trees and then what are they going to do? Start all over again with a Third Growth Festival? One thing I know for damned sure, by then there won't be enough bears left around there to make a bucket of soup, let alone a stew. Bear Festival, indeed! By damn, if I could round up enough of my kinfolk I'd organize a 'People Festival' based on the same principles."

I avoided eye contact with my friend, knowing that it would only encourage him to continue the filibuster.

"Ralph," I ventured. "I hate to keep bringing this up, but I really must get home. Your story touches me deeply. The citizens of McCleary are clearly very insensitive about bears. Perhaps some day I'll put you on a leash and we could go back down there and have a town meeting or something. You could lecture them on your side of the picture – explain things from the bear perspective. You could win them over with your great charm and show them the error of their ways."

Ralph had overexerted himself. He sat down heavily and rolled over on his back, legs all aspraddle. It was almost as if he had been pumping himself up and had suddenly sprung a leak.

"God, how naïve," he muttered.

"Have you got a VCR, Ralph?" I asked, knowing it was probably a dumb question.

"That's a pretty dumb question, don't you think? Where would I plug the damned thing in?"

"You seem to have ways of doing everything else," I replied.

"You been watching too many cartoons on TV," said Ralph

wearily. "What's with the VCR business?"

"They've got a videotape down at the library that tells all about the SG&BF," I said. "I've seen it and it might interest you to know that a lot of citizens in McCleary are plainly embarrassed about eating bear stew. Some of them even say that it tastes awful."

"They probably got into the batch with the horse in it."

The bear closed his eyes and fell silent. I thought perhaps he was about to go to sleep. That would be the last thing I needed; I might never get home.

"Well, Ralph," I said with a note of petulance. "I'm not getting any drier sitting up here and I've decided I don't really care much how you got that notch out of your ear. If you will be kind enough to point me in the right compass direction I will find my own way home. This drizzle isn't about to quit."

I stood up, brushed myself off and waited for some response.

"I never did find Loose Bessie," he mumbled. "But I found her friend Altogether Alice and she seemed pleased to see me." Ralph regarded me closely with a sparkle in his beady little eyes. He knew he had trapped me again.

"I'll probably wish I hadn't asked, but just what the hell is an Altogether Alice?"

Ralph straightened himself a bit and scratched his emaciated belly. "Altogether Alice, when she was younger, was considered the comeliest bruin in three counties. She had the prettiest haunches you ever did see. Had a face that could light up the densest huckleberry patch – nice manners, delicate habits. Everybody said she had it 'altogether,' so that's how she got the name. I used to hang around with her when I was younger but we kinda drifted apart when she took up with old Purple Lips Bartley, a contumelious old bastard who always had a bunch of dingle berries hanging off his hee-haw. Purple Lips was the kind of bear that gives us all a bad name. Never could figure out what Alice saw in the surly old bugger."

I'm afraid I let a bit of my frustration show.

"Contumelious?" I inquired with some annoyance. "What the hell is that?"

"Look it up," was Ralph's reply, which led me to believe that he didn't know what it meant either.

"Anyway, Alice told me that old Purple Lips got a little too big for his britches back in the winter of '91. He got caught rummaging around in the mayor's garbage can and ended up in the festival stew in the summer of '92. Seems like a long time to leave a carcass lying around if you ask me."

Altogether Alice was a comely little bruin.

"According to that videotape I told you about," I replied, "they hang their meat in the cold storage locker until they're ready to use it. Makes it more tender, they say."

"And I say they could have hung that churlish old malefactor in the 'tenderizing' locker for the rest of the century without effect. He had a heart as hard as anthracite coal and just as black. My God, did you know he tried to eat his own children?" Ralph spoke with a mixture of anger and sadness and not a little embarrassment. "Some of his activities make 'ethnic cleansing' sound like a picnic in the berry patch."

The trend of the conversation was causing me some uneasiness. The certain amount of research I had done on the habits of bears had led me to believe such things did happen, yet it was painful to think about. How does this square with lovable old Winnie the Pooh and all those cuddly Teddy Bears? At least it had deeply offended my friend Ralph, which gave me some comfort. Once again I felt a need to change the subject.

"Did you spend the winter with Alice?" I asked brightly.

"No, but not for lack of trying," he said. "I suggested we hibernate together, but she wasn't interested. I asked her to come back here and live with me but she said she had to stay down there where all her children were, even though they were all in constant danger from the stew meat hunters. Then the weather turned cold and she headed off to her hideout. Took me a while to find her place and when I did, I thought she might take pity on me, so I went into her cave and damned if she didn't throw me out. Couldn't reason with her. It was very embarrassing. Man, she sure picked up some bad habits from old Purple Lips. Scratched the devil out of me and took that big chunk out of my ear that's been worrying you so much. I got the feeling that she didn't want me around and I headed for home."

At last I knew the story of the notch and I wondered whether it had been worth the trouble.

"I'm a trifle disappointed, Ralph," I said. "I was expecting something a bit more melodramatic, like maybe a cougar attack or a run in with rednecks, or something."

Ralph snorted. "Ha! If you think an assault by an angry she-bear isn't hair-raising, you haven't been around much, friend. A cougar is a pussycat by comparison. Getting back home from McCleary was no walk in the park, either, but I get the feeling you're anxious to get out of the rain so I'll spare you the details and just hit the high spots."

"I'm grateful for your consideration," I said, hoping he would detect the sarcasm in my voice, but suspecting that he wouldn't. Ralph tends to become very wrapped up in himself when he tells a story.

"I made it across all the major highways without trouble. All but one, that is. I was moving at night, of course, and I made the mistake of not scouting out that stretch down by the old shingle mill. I sprinted across a couple of lanes and ran full tilt into one of those Jersey barrier things on the other side. I think I fractured my snout. I couldn't see where I was going and was just running to beat hell along the concrete when I heard what I knew was a rattletrap old pickup coming down the road.

"An alert bear gets so he can tell what kind of a thing is coming, you know. Old rattletrap pickups in the middle of the night are driven by rednecks full of beer. Guaranteed. Got big guns hanging behind the

seat. I thought I was done for. If they didn't get me with the guns, they'd come back and run over me. Figured I didn't have a chance. I hunkered down and waited for the bullets or the tires. But you know what? They didn't even see me! Their headlights were so dim, they didn't even see me.

"I could hear them singing bawdy songs inside that old '62 Chevy which was running on just a mini-

Then she took this chunk out of my ear.

mum of cylinders and they absolutely didn't even know I was there. Totally helpless I was, too, with my old ear wound bleeding all over me, snout all busted up, eyes full of tears, and backed up against that cold concrete. I figure I'm done for and up comes a picture in my brain where I'm hanging upside down in a McCleary cold storage locker. Move over Purple Lips, old R. Beauregard Shakesbear has come to keep you company."

The bear paused to catch his breath.

"A close call, Ralph, but clearly you survived this adventure. Do you think we could head down the hill now?"

It was as if he didn't hear me. He was gaining momentum again.

"You know what?" he asked. "You know what saved my life?"

"I haven't a clue." I said with resignation.

"That old truck wasn't full of rednecks, after all. It was a carload of brush pickers, all of the Hispanic persuasion, headed home to their camp full of cerveza – that's beer in Mexican, you know – and probably not even watching the road, let alone looking for bears. They don't bother us bears much anyway. We get along pretty good. It's a lucky thing, too, since we spend most of our time in the same territory. When I come across them out there picking stuff, I just sort of smile and go my own way.

"Once when I was going through a big huckleberry patch over by the power line I came right close to a bunch of them picking brush. One of them hollers 'ola, oso viejo,' which I find out later means 'Hello old bear' or some such and I come back with 'Que pasa, Jose' which is the only thing that I know in their lingo. Once I said 'hasta la visa' and they all ran like hell. I guess they thought I was asking for their visas or something. Anyway, it's a 'live and let live' thing between us. They probably know that messing around

70

with a bear can attract the authorities, which is the last thing they want to do, what with most of them being illegals and all."

"Fascinating," I said, hoping he would catch the tone of resignation in my voice. The concept of a smiling bear intrigued me, but I would pursue it some other time.

"Did you ever get across the highway?" I asked, hoping to get the story back on track.

"Yeah, I got around the Jersey barrier by feeling my way along. Then I found a little crick, got myself cleaned up, and washed my face so I could see again. Followed a deep gully down to the water where I ran along the beach most of the night until I got near Deer Creek, stirring up dogs all the way. Then I headed cross country 'til I got near old deaf whatshisname's place and I knew I was close to home. The hell of it was, it had started to snow and was getting mighty cold."

"This is beginning to sound like the Perils of Pauline," I muttered to myself. "He's probably about to run off a cliff."

"I headed straight for my winter quarters, dreaming of snug comfort for the rest of the winter. My God! Do you know what happened?" Ralph's face was contorted with emotion.

"I don't know, Ralph, but I wish you'd calm yourself. I'm not sure how much more of this excitement I can take." I noticed that it had stopped drizzling.

"My mother was living in my cave! She was in there with two cubs and taking up the whole damned space! I tried to squeeze myself in but the old biddy woke up like an erupting volcano and clawed the hell out of me, biting me severely on the butt and chasing me out in the snow. By the time I got out of there, the old ear wound and the broken snout were bleeding again and I had seriously lacerated buttocks. Jeez! My own mother! Oh, God, the indignity of

71

it all! Maybe now you know why I look so bad. I've had to spend the whole rest of the winter up in my tree, out in the cold. It's a wonder I'm not dead."

"I feel your pain, Ralph. Your story has touched me deeply, but soon the berries will be ripe again, and all will be right with the world. Now, really, I must get back down the hill. Please lead the way."

Ralph arose slowly as though the telling of his story had caused him further physical distress.

"I thought I might have gotten a little more sympathy and compassion," he said glumly. "This hasn't been easy, you know."

The bear moved slowly out of the small clearing through the thick huckleberry bushes. Interestingly enough, he went in exactly the opposite direction that I would have chosen. I guessed it was best that I had listened to his whole long story for had I left on my own there is no telling where I would have ended up. We proceeded in a generally westerly direction until I began to recog-

I feel your pain, Ralph.

nize familiar landmarks. Soon we arrived at our old berry patch rendezvous.

Ralph sat down wearily. "I'm going back to see if Mother Ophelia has vacated my sanctuary yet. Dammit, she has her own cave. She can take my two little step-siblings off to her own place. It's time she began their Shakespeare education, anyway. I need rest."

A *Comedy of Errors* might be a good place to start, I thought to myself. Or maybe *The Taming of the Shrew*.

The bear got slowly to all fours and he was a sorry sight. Even though most of his wounds had healed to a degree, his emaciated condition gave him the appearance of a desperately ill old bruin. I felt sure that with an improved diet he would soon begin to return to his old self, but the slightly bent nose and the notch out of his ear would be permanent reminders of his "winter of discontent."

About the time I was ready to head back down the hill I thought of the matter of the statue and the sign. I wasn't sure this would be a good time to bring it up, what with all the misfortunes he had been through, but decided to remind him about it anyway.

"Say, Ralph," I said seriously. "I finished the statue. It looks good. The sign's all set to go, too."

The old bear looked at me dimly and I felt a moment of unease. Had he forgotten the arrangement we had made? I guessed this might not be the best time to pursue the matter. Shucks, I could find a few quotations on my own, I decided. Get 'em off T-shirts and bumper stickers until the old reprobate recovered his health.

"I'll wait until you get your strength back," I said. "And for God's sake try to stay out of trouble. I'll leave some grub for you down on the trail. Watch for it or the raccoons will get to it before you do."

"A six-pack or two would be nice. It really restores the spirits and I happen to know that raccoons don't like beer."

I was some distance down the trail when I heard his voice.

"Don't forget, longnecks. They've got to be longnecks."

SPEED READING IS TAUGHT HERE

DRIVE CAREFULLY WE NEED ALL THE TAXPAYERS WE CAN GET

IT'S AWFULLY HARD TO GET ANY SLEEP OUT HERE

QUIET

IF YOU DRIVE LIKE HELL, YOU'RE BOUND TO GET THERE

STOP READING THIS AND WATCH THE ROAD

SLOW READERS PLEASE WATCH THE ROAD

?

PEOPLE SAY I TALK TOO FAST

Once I persuaded Ralph to let me organize a Highway Speed Reduction Campaign. Won't do any good," he said. "Those hotshots are going too fast to read the signs. You're just wasting ink."

CHAPTER SIX
Macduff

It was the middle of summer before I heard anything further from Ralph. Quite frankly, I hadn't been looking for him since I had plenty to do without the kind of distractions he invariably created. I managed to keep the bear sign changed at reasonable intervals but, to be honest, the task of finding new and clever – especially clever – quotations to display was becoming more and more burdensome. I began to have an uneasy feeling that the old curmudgeon was trying to swindle me, but since I remembered him telling me not to go looking for him unless the signal was displayed in the stump, I decided to follow instructions. Nevertheless, I resolved to let him know the next time I saw him that I was going to break the contract, as he called it, if he didn't live up to his end of the deal.

Then, on a morning in the second week of July, the flag appeared in the stump and I interrupted work on a carving of a large, leaping salmon to go see what the old scoundrel wanted. I knew that Ralph would be pleased to see that I hadn't forgotten to bring along the six-pack of his favorite longnecks.

The new crop of berries hadn't really begun to ripen, so I didn't expect to find my friend in the patch. Sure enough, he was down the hill a bit, vigorously tearing at a large rotten log. As I approached, he raised his massive head, scrinched his little eyes half-closed and lifted his eyebrows. I took this to be a sign of greeting.

"*Que pasa*, old buddy," he rumbled happily. "By damn, I'm getting you properly trained. Beer goes wonderfully well with fresh ants."

"Sit down here and let's talk." He indicated a small stump, which at the time was overrun with terrified insects.

"I'll stand, if you don't mind," I said. "I have an aversion to bugs running around in my britches. You're looking good, Ralph, a whole lot better than the last time I saw you. Been getting plenty to eat?"

I had to wait for an answer while he attended to the business of pursuing bugs with a tongue which suddenly seemed much too long to fit in his mouth. I watched in fascination as ants by the hundreds disappeared, accompanied by loud smacking and slobbering noises. A goodly number of the insects escaped his tongue and could be seen running around in confusion on his nose and face. Paying them no heed, he continued his clawing and rummaging until it appeared that the number of fleeing ants was noticeably reduced. Backing away from the log the bear sneezed twice with great vigor, discharging several insects from his nose with the force of BBs from an air gun. He lowered his head and shook himself with such force that I'm certain all four feet came off the ground. Debris flew in every direction and in an instant his coat took on a shining elegance. My friend was positively

Termites & beer
... a hard-to-beat combination.

pristine, his black fur luminous in the morning sunlight.

Ralph hadn't gained back all the weight he had lost in his winter adventures; his snout still seemed a little off kilter since his collision with the Jersey barrier, but the hair had grown over the notch in his ear and the old fellow looked pretty much his original self.

He backed up to the stump, seated himself and crossed his legs in that familiar pose that I had long since become accustomed to. The thought went through my mind that this might just be the only bear in the whole world who sits that way.

"Well, now," said Ralph with a contented sigh. "Suppose you twist the cap off one of those Buds so I can wash down the termites."

Ralph seemed to make no distinction between ants and ter- mites. He used the terms interchangeably.

"Open one for yourself and sit down – take the weight off. How's it been going with you?" he asked cheerily.

I determined not to let him get too comfortable before I let him know of my displeasure about the sign deal.

"Gee, thanks," I said, with barely disguised sarcasm. "I get invited to have one of my own beers and sit down when there's nothing to sit on. You're too kind, Ralph."

Ralph seemed genuinely chagrined.

"Oh, sorry old boy," he said, springing to his feet and making a big to-do of brushing off the stump. "Here, take mine. The ants are all gone and the seat's clean. I'll get another one."

He vanished through a tangle of huckleberry bushes. I could hear him thrashing about in the underbrush, humming loudly to himself. Sounds like Yogi Bear, I thought, and wondered if humming was a bear trait. Another thing to remember to ask him sometime. He re- turned walking upright on his hind legs and carrying a large log in his two front paws as easily as though it were a piece of kindling.

"Here we go," he said, plopping the log down. "Now let's get started on that beer. I've got a powerful thirst. Termites are a mite salty."

Perhaps I haven't mentioned it before, but a bear has a particular problem when it comes to holding small objects. A beer bottle is a good example. It's a two-handed operation which requires a hand (paw) on each side of the bottle and enough opposing pressure to keep it from sliding out. Ralph's problem was similar to that which a small child has in drinking from a bottle before its hands are large enough to get a one-handed grip. Ralph had no trouble mastering the technique once he got the bottle picked up, but he didn't always get it centered properly in his mouth with the result that sometimes the contents came pouring out in unexpected places. Such was the case today. In his haste to get on with the drinking he failed to pay attention to details and managed to dump a goodly portion of his beer all over his ample belly. In trying to get his head tipped properly, he bent so far over backwards that he ended up on his back on the ground with his legs hanging over the log. By now the beer was gone – some of it probably down his throat, but mostly all over his front. For a creature who was so graceful in other ways, this bear became a positive clod in the art of drinking from a bottle. I resolved never to take him into a saloon.

"Well," he said sheepishly. "That was a good sample, but I'm going to need a bit more to get a real taste. I'd be obliged if you'd twist the top off another one and just hand it to me while I'm here in the right position.""

"This whole thing looks like the comedy act in a Russian circus," I observed, unable to help myself.

"Funny you should mention that," he said cheerily. "I've often considered joining a circus where I'd have three squares a day, nobody shooting at me, and no dogs chasing me up the trees. All in exchange for doing a few tricks each day. Sounds like a deal that has possibilities. How can I get in touch with them?"

"Let's be serious, Ralph," I said. "We've got some important matters to discuss."

"Let me finish the beer first. It's hard to be serious when I'm in this position." In one continuous gulp the beer was gone, successfully this time.

Ralph rolled over onto his stomach and assumed the posture of a big dog: two paws out front, his head resting between them and his expression eager, as if he were waiting for me to throw a stick for him to fetch. His eyes sparkled playfully. This was clearly a bear who was back in good health.

"I'm ready to be serious," he said.

It seemed to me that this was probably not exactly true. I think those two beers had gone straight to his head. Either that or ants had a salubrious effect on bears. Maybe it was the beer mixed with the bugs. I made a mental note to ask him about this sometime, too.

"Okay, Ralph, here's the problem. Do you remember the deal we made way back over a year ago? Back when I said I'd carve a statue of you in the chair?"

"Yeah, kinda, what about it?"

"Well, tell me what the deal was," I said, trying to put a little hardness in my voice like I was back teaching school and suggesting to some sophomore malingerer that he had missed another important assignment.

"You make a statue of me sitting in a chair holding a sign," Ralph said dreamily. "How's about we have another beer?"

I ignored the request. "What's going to be on the sign?" I asked.

"Shoot, I don't know. Funny stuff like, 'THE OTHER DAY A DOG PEED ON MY FOOT?' That comes from H.L. Mencken, I think. Or, 'I DON'T BUY BEER I JUST RENT IT.' There's lots of good Shakespeare stuff, too. How about 'STAY ON THE WINDY SIDE OF CARE,' *Much Ado About Nothing*, Act Two. Maybe 'HARKEN, THE INAUDIBLE AND NOISLESS FOOT OF TIME' from *All's Well That Ends Well*, Scene 4. Sounds redundant, I know, but old Bill always wanted to make sure he got his message across, whatever the hell it might be. What about 'IF YOU CAN'T BEAT 'EM HAVE THEM JOIN YOU?' I made that one up myself."

"Ralph," I said, my voice rising. "Since I put that wooden bear out on the highway I have had to think up over one hundred-fifty clever things to put on that sign. I've had to do it all by myself. That wasn't the deal, you know. You said *you* would think up the stuff. I was just supposed to write the signs. You're not living up to your part of the bargain, Ralph, and I'm sick of having to do all the work. Either you start doing your share, my friend, or I'm going down there and saw the head off that damned statue and make firewood out of it. I'm pissed off in case you haven't noticed. I thought

81

even a dumb bear would have more consideration. A deal's a deal you know. Am I going to have to get you to sign a written contract to get you to live up to your bargain?"

Suddenly I had the feeling that maybe I was pushing my luck. Ralph was getting slowly to his feet – his hind feet – which usually meant that he was upset about something. He towered above me, slowly leaning down until his enormous snout was within inches of my face and I began to understand how an ant must feel.

"Calm yourself, old man," he said evenly. "You've gotten yourself all red in the face. You do remember what Mark Twain said, don't you?"

"Probably," I said cautiously. "But tell me anyway."

"That wise old gent said, 'Humans are the only animal that blushes or has a need to.' Put that on your sign down there."

Even though I knew this wasn't the very best time for a riposte, I wasn't going to let the old reprobate get the best of me.

"Do you know what Edward Young had to say on the same subject?" I asked.

"No, I don't even know who Edward Young is."

"He said, 'The man that blushes is not quite a brute.'"

Ralph regarded me with a look of annoyance. "Enough of the one-upsmanship – let's try to stick to the subject. You're the one who's always complaining about losing focus. Suppose you shut up for awhile and listen to what I have to say. And I think it best if we leave the word 'brute' out of our conversation, too. It's insensitive."

Oh, my God, I thought. I never expected to hear that word coming from my curmudgeonly friend. I well remember listening to this very same bear, in a conversation which I had cataloged in my notes as "Tirade on Political Correctness," pledge never to use the word "insensitive" in any context. Could the old bugger be losing his grip?

"Well, I'm sorry if I offended you," I said with mock contriteness.

"I know what you're thinking," said Ralph, fixing me with a strangely serene look. "Don't get the idea that I'm going soft in the head, but I had an experience last week that has set me to thinking about a lot of things. If you've got a few minutes I'll tell you about it."

"Please don't change the subject, my friend," I said with some heat. "I came up here to get this sign matter resolved and that's what I intend to do. Don't try to get me off track. I know only too well your ability to obfuscate things. You can tell me about your new experience some other time. Focus, man, focus! What do you intend to do about the sign business?"

Ralph sighed wearily, "Yes, of course, focus. But please don't say 'focus, man, focus.' I'm a bear and the last thing I ever intend to be is a man, so say 'focus, bear, focus,' if you must. And while we're on the subject, I've often wondered why you people have to add the word 'man' in all your sentences. Is this some kind of cultural thing? You know I'd be able to focus much better if you'll give me another of those beers."

Trying to appear nonchalant and calm, I did as I was directed, but I'm sure Ralph didn't miss the slight tremble of my hand as I handed him the bottle.

"The use of the word 'man' is a fixation of the younger generation," I offered, "and is used, I suspect, as a substitute for thought or to compensate for a lack of basic vocabulary. How the hell do I know? I belong to the older generation – actually the old generation. Geez!"

I knew I had to get him back on course before he was off on some new tangent.

Ralph finished his beer, wiped his chin on his forearm, carefully replaced the empty bottle in the carton and eased himself down on the ground. He seated himself with his back to a small tree, and sighed deeply.

"Okay, my friend," he said, fixing me with his beady gaze. "We will now do some intense focusing. Let's see if we can sort out our problem here."

I suddenly felt like a patient on the psychiatrist's couch and I began to wonder who had the problem. As a matter of fact I began to question just what the problem was. Holding a conversation with a bear has a singular way of scrambling one's attention – like watching a chicken walk backwards or a raccoon hold up a liquor store. It's disconcerting. Sometimes the subject matter gets lost in the confusion.

"Alright," said my furry friend from his comfortable position. "Let's start with a basic anatomy lesson. In your usually inattentive way you've probably never noticed that there is a considerable difference in the way people and bears are constructed. I want you to take a careful look at these."

Ralph held out his massive paws. "Very useful for many purposes to be sure; great for dislocating termites, climbing trees, upsetting beehives, and all kinds of heavy lifting, but hardly de-signed for some of the tasks you seem to think I should be capable of, like writing signs and such."

"I didn't say you had to *write* the signs, damn it, but you agreed to think them up. I'll write the signs. As I recall it was your suggestion to get your ideas out to the masses, which, now that I think of it, makes you sound like some kind of communist commissar. All you have to do is put 'em in a list for me," I said heatedly. "You having second thoughts?"

"I think that is exactly where our problem lies," said Ralph wearily. "To coin an old phrase, 'the spirit is willing, but the flesh is weak.' You've got a pencil in your pocket, there, throw it over. I want to show you something."

I tossed the pencil across to the bear. It landed close to his hind foot and I immediately began to see why bears don't normally take up work in the writing profession. Ralph began a concentrated effort to pick up the pencil between those great big yellow claws of his. He pursued it back and forth between his legs trying to capture it between his "fingers". He finally scooped it up and had it lying in his paw but could do nothing more with it until he took it in his mouth where, in trying to maneuver it so that the lead end would point forward, managed to snap it in two.

"Bears are not good at delicate tasks," said Ralph wearily. "We lack dexterity. Has something to do with the opposable thumb, I think. Darwin spoke about it at some length in connection with monkeys."

I began to feel some embarrassment. Why hadn't I thought of this?

"So, then," said Ralph, "in the words of the Bard, 'Here's the rub.' Either you are going to have to climb the hill and let me dictate

Bears are not good at delicate tasks.

my wittcisms to you, or we'll have to find somebody to act as our secretary who can write them out and then bring them down to you. Who that might be I have no idea. There's nobody up here that I know of who's smart enough to handle a job like that except maybe Macduff, and he's pretty young."

"Macduff? Who's Macduff?"

"Macduff is my great-grandson. At least I *think* he's my great-grandson. Maybe he's a great-grandcousin or a nephew or something like that. I'm not strong on relationships, but with a name like Macduff he's got to be

Macduff, Ralph's orphaned great grandson, as he looked when I first met him.

a Shakesbear. He belongs in the family somehow and he seems pretty smart. Maybe we can teach him to write."

Oh, my God, not another talking bear, I thought. What next?

"How come I haven't met him?" I asked with suspicion. "Where does this Macduff bear hang out?"

"At the moment, right up in that tree," said Ralph, pointing to a nearby hemlock. "I was teaching him how to hunt termites when we heard you come puffing up the hill. Sent him up the tree until I was sure it was really you. It's good training for a cub, practicing evasion skills."

Ralph made a peculiar popping noise with his mouth.

"Come on down Duffy, meet the old man. There's no danger. He's difficult, but he's completely harmless."

From around the trunk of the tree, about twenty feet from the ground, appeared a small furry bundle which looked like the head of a medium-sized black dog. Quick as a wink, my brain processed a lot of stored information. Dogs don't climb trees so that creature up there must be a cub bear. There really was a similarity to a dog, to be sure, but I could see that the ears weren't quite dog-like. More of the head appeared with black eyes sparkling and ears cocked alertly. Even at an instant glance there was an unmistakable sign of deviltry. Suddenly the head vanished and I heard scraping noises, which indicated that the cub was backing down the trunk, tearing off chunks of loose bark as he descended. In a second the head appeared again at ground level, looking quizzically at Ralph.

"Yes, come on out, come on out. There's no danger," said my friend.

The cub sprinted across the clearing, scurried behind Ralph and then peered around the older bear's immense bulk, still wearing that endearing look of intelligence and mischief. This, I thought to myself, is where the idea for those cuddly, stuffed Teddy Bears came from.

Little Macduff had the typical brown muzzle and eyebrow markings that give very young black bears a look of whimsy and childish curiosity. Splashed across his small chest was a white marking in the shape of an inverted crescent. Macduff wouldn't be difficult to identify in a crowd, I thought. My recent anger at old Ralph had melted away in the presence of this cuddly bundle of fur. It took effort to bring myself back to reality and I tried not to look at his needle sharp claws. I couldn't help thinking that they probably weren't a bit duller than a cougar's claws. I resolved to resist the temptation to get in a rough-house session with Junior.

Ralph cleared his throat and began a little speech that, even though I had become accustomed to his guttural, rumbling diction, was even harder to understand than usual. I guessed it may have been some sort of bear shorthand, the kind of regional dialect used among cultural groups which is not always intelligible to outsiders. As nearly as I could tell, this is what he said:

"Macduff, I'm sure you've seen these kinds of creatures before, but probably not this close up. This is what is called a human being. The scientific name is *Homo sapiens*. It almost always walks on its hind legs, but can't run very fast. While you are never in danger of being overtaken in a footrace, the human being is a devious creature and many of them cannot be trusted. Some carry firearms which they use to kill other creatures. Humans seem to have a particular need to kill each other, but as a second choice they are fond of shooting bears, which they consider untrustworthy and dangerous."

"This specimen here," he said pointing to me, "does not carry a firearm and I have found him to be trustworthy and not dangerous."

Here Ralph's voice went almost to a whisper, but I think what I heard him say was, "He's not smart at all and doesn't know diddly-squat about getting around in the woods, so I help him when I can. He has very peculiar ideas about most everything, but I'll tell you about that later."

Ralph's voice then resumed its former volume. "I'm sure your mother, rest her soul, has taught you to stay away from human beings and also to avoid their pets, the dogs, who get most of their ideas from humans and who thus are also afraid of bears. Dogs can't climb trees, so you are safe up in one, but dogs are very noisy and obstreperous – you might want to look that word up – and they attract humans who carry firearms and who think it's some kind of manly act to shoot a bear, especially when it's up in a tree." Ralph paused to catch his breath.

I couldn't resist a rejoinder. "You've lost your thread as usual. We were talking about my problem, remember? Tell the cub about the signs, Ralph. Ask him if he knows how to write."

"All things in good time, my friend, all things in good time."

Macduff disappeared behind Ralph again, then tugged on the older bear's ear, causing Ralph to lower his head to the point where the cub could speak into it. Some sort of short, whispered conversation took place which I was not able to hear.

"The cub wants to know why you don't have any fur on your head. What should I tell him?"

"Oh, my God," I blurted. "Tell him I pulled it all out trying to hold intelligent conversations with his grandfather. Macduff, come over and sit by me and tell me about yourself."

The small head reappeared. The cub looked at the older bear quizzically, seeking direction.

"Sure, go ahead, Duffy. Like I said, he's harmless. Excitable, but not dangerous. Tell him anything he wants to know - except where we live, that is."

Slowly, the little fellow eased himself out from behind his grandfather. He

Macduff

89

moved tentatively toward me, then looked back at Ralph, still unsure that this was the right thing to do.

"Go on, son, there's no danger. If he tries any funny stuff I'll eat him. That might be the best thing to do anyway. That would take care of his sign problem."

"Your grandpa is a great kidder, Macduff. He told me a long time ago he didn't eat people. That is true, isn't it?" I asked with only a slight twinge of concern.

The little bear cautiously sat on the ground next to my stump, never taking his eyes off Ralph. I could see a slight quiver go through his small body. Ralph was across the way trying to use his teeth to wrench the cap off the last beer.

"Don't be afraid son, your gramps is right. I do not harm other creatures. I had a bear that looked just about like you when I was little. His name was Linklighter. My brother and I had him for ten years until all the sawdust finally leaked out of him. He wasn't as big as you are.

"You can talk, can't you Macduff?"

This is the usual sparkling repartee I use when conversing with small children.

He made no reply. I decided to address Ralph as a way of breaking the tension.

"Dammit, Ralph, if you'll bring that bottle over here I'll take the cap off for you."

Just then he spit out the cap explosively, apparently having finally mastered the technique, and was now back to working on his two-handed consumption grip.

"Keep your eye on your grandpa," I said to Macduff. "Unless I miss my guess, he's about to tip over backward."

90

I was wrong. The old bear performed the drinking maneuver flawlessly, remaining perfectly upright on his log.

"Way to go, Ralph. Well done! You're finally catching on."

It was then that I first heard the piping voice of little Macduff, clear as could be. No slurring of words, no guttural mutterings.

"I'm not full of sawdust," he said.

I was taken aback with astonishment. I looked across at Ralph, but he was still chugging his Budweiser, totally oblivious of what was going on between me and the cub bear. I tried to compose myself.

"I'm sorry, I didn't mean to suggest that you were. I know better than that," I said.

Duffy looked at me like he wasn't convinced. "Okay," he said.

I felt that I had to keep the conversation going so I resorted to the usual questions that all old people ask when talking to small children.

"What grade are you in, Duffy? You do go to school don't you? Have you learned how to write yet? It's all right if I call you Duffy, isn't it?"

The cub was still watching his grandfather who was now pursuing ants again.

"None, no, yes, that's cool," was the cub's response.

I realized that I would have to change my tactics. This was a small bear of very few words and one question at a time looked like the best approach. In any case, I had to go back and see if I could remember the order in which I had asked the first ones.

— I'm not full of sawdust ...

Let's see: What grade? None. School? No. Can write? Yes. Self-taught? Apparently. Name? Cool, which is younger generation talk for "okay."

While I was figuring all this out, young Duffy had run back over and was busily clawing at the log with his grandfather. I think he had already forgotten me.

"Hey, Ralph! Good news! The boy says he can write."

"Fine," said the old bear in his slobbery way, "but he hasn't got anything to write on, or with either, for that matter. You'll have to outfit him with supplies."

I walked over to the ant dispersal operation and squatted down next to little Macduff who was now clearly less apprehensive about my presence.

"Duffy," I said, using my small person voice. "Do you think you can help your old grandpa and me out with this problem? Can you write down stuff for him and bring it down to me, like we were talking about?"

"Winnie the Pooh was full of sawdust. Do you know what a Pooh is?" asked Duffy, and then promptly answered his own question.

"He was a bear with no brains. Pooh is bear talk for 'not smart.' That's not explained in the book."

While I was pleased to learn that the small bear could actually put complete sentences together, I was getting the uneasy feeling that young Macduff might have the same "focus problem" as his grandfather. Come to think of it, I thought, Winnie the Pooh had the same trait. Could this be a basic flaw in the bear character?

"I'm not sure I ever knew what a Pooh is, or was," I said. "If I ever did know, I have forgotten. Maybe I could look it up."

"No need, Dude. I just told you what a Pooh Bear is. Geez."

"I beg your pardon," I said with some shock, troubled by what appeared to be the sudden lack of respect from this small creature who but a moment before was so shy and reticent. I looked to Ralph for help.

"Meet the younger generation," said the older bear. "They pick up that stuff from the TV."

"Duffy, apologize to the old guy, please. He comes from several generations back when they used to be fond of expressions like, 'children should be seen but not heard,' which really means 'don't trouble me with new ideas, the old ones are better.'"

"Sorry, Dude, want some termites? New crop. Fresh and very tender. Try 'em."

"His kind don't eat termites, Duffy," said Ralph. "Not around here, anyway. It's just as well. If they liked them they would have cleaned them all out by now, like the fish."

"I wonder if we can get back to the matter I came up here about," I said with a touch of impatience. "Ralph, can we get the boy to do our paper work?"

"I don't speak for the lad. Ask him yourself. It's time he began making his own decisions."

"What about it, Duff? Think you can help out your old Grandpa? Write stuff for him?"

"Devise, wit; write, pen; for I am whole volumes in folio, Dude. We must take the current where it serves or lose our ventures. Bring on your witticisms, sire, and I will transcribe them faithfully. Fear not my nature for it is too full of the milk of human kindness, man."

Ralph was now backed up to a small tree scratching his rump, a dreamy look on his face.

"What in God's name is the boy saying, Ralph? Help me out. What kind of lingo is that?" I asked.

"Sounds like mangled Shakespeare to me. That 'milk of human kindness' stuff comes from *Macbeth*. Who knows what the rest of it is. The boy had to quit his lessons when his mother disappeared so he's got stuff all mixed up."

"Hey, Duffy. Use plain English when you're talking to the old man. He doesn't savvy the Bard."

"What I'm trying to say, Dude, is bring on the humor. Duff will write your stuff."

I was just beginning to think we might have reached some sort of understanding on how we were going to proceed when things began to go off track again. The bears started to set working conditions. In addition to the writing supplies he required, Macduff demanded that I bring lunch for everybody whenever I came up to get the quotations and then damned if Ralph didn't pipe up with an insistence on a six-pack of beer. He really wanted two six-packs, but I told him no dice.

"One is the absolute limit," I said. "I'm going to have to put on a backpack as it is and I'm damned if I can carry that kind of a load up that miserable trail. And I'm just about to call this whole deal off. I think I'll just go down there and put one more quotation on your damnable sign. Something like, 'OH THE HELL WITH IT. I QUIT!'"

I heard a piping little voice behind me say, "You're right,

Grandpa, he is a difficult old fart."

I was about to reply to the little wisecracker with some suitably invidious comment when I noticed the hair on Ralph's neck rise ominously, the furred animal's universal sign of alarm and danger. I immediately felt an instinctive alarm of my own. I knew that had I any hair on the back of my neck, it too, would have risen, even though I couldn't have known for what reason. I heard a low, throaty growl from Ralph who whirled on his hind legs and cuffed little Duffy with such force that the cub rolled like a lopsided ball toward the exit to our clearing.

Instantly he was back on his feet, Ralph right behind him applying well-placed swats to his galloping backsides, forcing him to maintain his best speed. In an instant they were gone and I was alone in the clearing, standing dumbstruck in astonishment at the abruptness of their departure.

My first thought was that Ralph was punishing Duffy for his disrespectful remark, but this was totally out-of-character. To be sure, Ralph's persona was based on a high level of disrespect, especially toward people which he considered an inferior species, but Ralph knew me well enough to know that I could hold my own with wisecracking juveniles. Anyway, Macduff was more amusing than disparaging. I enjoyed the riposte with both of them.

Nevertheless, I knew something serious had spooked the old bear and it was with a touch of uneasiness that I began tidying up our recent meeting place. I had barely finished putting the empty bottles back in the carton and picking up bottle caps when the reason for Ralph's sudden departure strode into view.

CHAPTER SEVEN
The Unnatural Naturalist

I was just beginning to get used to having a talking bear practically in my back yard when a new creature arrived to put further strain on my overtaxed credulity. At least this new arrival was human – sort of – which made him more acceptable, although no less unique. Later on, when I was trying to describe this character to Ralph, he asked me to write up a description of our meeting. He said he'd seen the guy out in the woods several times and wanted to know who and what he was. This is what I wrote:

A DESCRIPTION OF ODDWARE B. STUMPLE,
A NEW-AGE NATURALIST
WRITTEN FOR RALPH B. SHAKESBEAR, A BEAR
(To the best of my recollection)

The thing that suddenly appeared in our little clearing, and what had spooked you and Duffy into your abrupt departure, was what looked like a six-foot-tall, nearsighted, praying mantis dressed in a scoutmaster's outfit. He had a backpack with stuff hanging all over it and he was doing an excellent imitation of Teddy Roosevelt on a campaign trip, working the crowd for votes.

Grinning broadly, he strode vigorously across the clearing, hand outstretched exclaiming, "Splendid, splendid. Wonderful to find a fellow traveler so far from the pother of civilization, and one after my own heart, picking up litter left by our less tidy citizens. What a noble thing!"

"Oddware. B. Stumple is my name. I'm on independent study from The Evergreen State College doing self-directed research on animal and insect distribution in the western part of our state with ancillary investigation into environmental factors pertaining to preservation of endangered and threatened species."

He still had his hand outstretched waiting to shake hands I supposed, but I stood there mute, in a state of minor shock, with my mouth hanging open. I finally shifted the carton of empties to my other side and took the proffered hand.

Well, it wasn't Teddy Roosevelt after all, I decided. The handshake was too limp. As he shrugged himself out of his backpack and fussed with various items of his equipment, I had an opportunity to gather my wits and observe my visitor more carefully.

No wonder you vanished in such a hurry, Ralph! This was a *Homo sapiens* of a decidedly different stripe.

Oddware Stumple clearly suffered from poor eyesight, not helped any by the fact that the thick lenses of his spectacles seemed in need of a good scrubbing. In fact, the whole eyeglass assembly seemed to be homemade, held together by bits of duct tape and wire.

Looking at Stumple from dead-ahead was like looking at a smiling owl through old plexiglas. He wore a long-billed baseball cap whose best years were long gone and which was covered with an astonishing assortment of colorful buttons and emblems. The one displayed most prominently – right in the front – was a picture of a sad-looking cow surrounded by the words "BOYCOTT LEATHER." To right and left were "HONOR MOTHER EARTH" and "FREE TIBET." I could see "FISH FIRST!" on one side, but the others would have to wait because the hat itself caught my attention. It was slightly too big for his head and pulled down too far, causing his ears to splay out, which seldom lends itself to promoting a look of intelligence.

Although O.B. Stumple had a splendid ponytail flowing from under the cap and secured neatly by a rubber band, his facial hair would have been an embarrassment to Yasser Arafat. He wore baggy camouflaged shorts with lots of pockets and long khaki stockings folded down at the top, scoutmaster style. Huge clodhopper boots were incongruously out-of-place on the end of his spider-like legs. A clipboard and a pair of Birkenstock sandals were tied to the top of his bulging backpack.

Every new observation pointed to the unmistakable fact that I was in the presence of a full-blown environmental activist, awash in dreamy causes and idealistic nonsense, but I didn't know that any of them were still flogging that old "Free Tibet" horse.

You'd be interested in this, Ralph. I remembered how you often lectured me about dreamers tilting at foreign windmills when they should have been working on local problems where they had a chance of being successful, and once demanded that I get a bunch of "SAVE THE BEARS" bumper stickers made up to take down to McCleary. And you continue to insist that I put "SAVE THE BEARS" up on your sign every week or two even though I don't.

Stumple was fussing with the fastenings on his backpack when I spied a Budweiser bottle cap that I had overlooked. It was the one you had discarded when you went ass-over-teakettle. I picked it up and put it in the carton and Stumple went rhapsodic. I thought he

was going to kiss me. Lord, God, it doesn't take much to excite these people, I thought.

"It's so refreshing to find someone who takes the stewardship of the land seriously," Stumple gushed. He had taken a small notebook from his pocket. "Down at TESC we have an honor roll of names of people who are sensitive to the needs of the earth. I would like to nominate you for membership. Can I have your name?" His pencil was poised.

"Ah, shucks," I said modestly. "You don't have to do that." Little did he know that I was just cleaning up after a slobbish black bear.

I told him my name was Ralph Beauregard. "Forgive my ignorance," I asked, "but what is a TESC?"

Stumple smiled serenely. "That's our nickname for The Evergreen State College. As the old saying goes 'She's a small school but there are those of us who love her.'"

Lord, God, it doesn't take much to excite these people.

"TESC is catchy. Has a nice lilt to it." I tried to sound sincere although I'm not sure I was successful.

"Did you know that our school mascot is the geoduck? We have an admirable sense of humor, don't you think, Ralph?"

Oddware began removing things from his backpack including several notebooks, a rolled-up pair of stockings, two squashed Coors Lite cans, and something that looked like a surveyor's instrument.

"It's a crime how careless some of our fellows can be," he went on in a disjointed monologue. "They seem to have absolutely given up caring for the planet. So I make it a habit, during my travels, of cleaning up what I can and at least taking note of where there are pockets of rubbish so that when we have the resources to enter into a general cleanup, I will have the locations accurately pinpointed on my maps." He opened one of his notebooks.

"Would you believe that just since yesterday I have documented two unauthorized dump sites, one with a Whirlpool washing machine, and another with a kitchen range, a queen-size mattress and what appeared to be a perfectly good commode? It's an absolute disgrace! And would you believe that yesterday I came across the remains of an old Essex automobile? I could still make out the name on it. I counted eighty-seven bullet holes in it before I gave up. Would you believe it?"

"A lot of people didn't like the Essex," I said, doing my best to sound serious. What I really felt was a need to interrupt the filibuster and perhaps get in a dig at one of Oddware's causes at a single stroke.

"I say, are you making any progress on the Tibet issue?" I asked solemnly.

He peered at me blankly, blinking several times.

"The button on your cap," I said, pointing.

"Oh, yes, of course. Tibet. Yes, yes, the work goes on. Our cause is just and we will prevail. Money is short, of course. I send them what I can. Would you like to help?" he asked earnestly. "With every one hundred dollar contribution you get one of the buttons and a sticker to put on your bumper. It's a wonderful crusade."

"I'm afraid I'm a bit stretched at the moment," I said, trying to project the idea that otherwise it was one of my favorite issues. This was my first experience in actually seeing a "Free Tibet" person in the flesh and I had to admit he was an exact fit for all my mental images of what one looked like. I just knew that Oddware B. Stumple had an old Volkswagen camper parked someplace nearby and that there would be a "Free Tibet" sticker on it, too. That was certain.

I noticed Stumple squinting with great concentration at the rotten log that you and Macduff had been clawing at.

"Oh, my goodness," he exclaimed in excitement. "There have been bears here. See the marks on that log? A bear has been hunting for ant grubs. Oh, what a splendid find!"

In an instant he was into his backpack again, rummaging through its contents. He brought forth a camera and began photographing the log from every angle, chattering with excitement. Then he unhooked his clipboard and commenced writing rapidly, making a sketch of the log with a bunch of arrows and symbols and what seemed to be a whole lot of detailed description. Then out came a large magnifying glass, through which he peered intently.

"See here," he said excitedly. "Here's a dead worker. These are the fire ants, *Solenopsis geminata*. This was a very large colony. The bear had a big meal here. Utterly splendid! What a fortuitous find!"

Stumple produced a small vial from his pack and commenced digging at the rotted log until he spooked a lone ant that you and Duffy had overlooked. He herded the insect into the vial, then held it up close to my face.

"This is the worker ant. Notice the large head, the incurved teeth, highly developed mandibles, and the long legs. They are fierce fighters, you know; they protect the colony from invaders."

"Don't you think maybe we ought to get out of here if there's bears around?" I asked, trying to put a note of apprehension in my voice.

"It's not likely that a bear will come back as long as we're here. This is your black bear, you know. *Ursus americanus*. Very shy and only a danger to people if cornered or when its young are threatened."

That's exactly what he said, Ralph. I hope you're not offended. It seems like everybody I run into knows the scientific name of the black bear. I tried to act surprised and interested. You would have been proud of me, Ralph. I didn't tell him I already know all I need to know about black bears.

As Stumple knelt down beside the log I noticed that the soles on his boots appeared to have been fashioned from truck tires which were probably attached with super glue or epoxy. Still got lots of miles on 'em, I thought.

He was writing rapidly in a spiral notebook as he continued. "I would estimate that this colony was of at least 100,000 magnitude which would have been a providential find for any bear. This time of year, before the berries ripen, bears are constantly on the lookout for edible insects."

Also for their favorite beer, I thought.

It was then that I noticed several more buttons on the back side of his cap. There was EARTH FIRST!, SIERRA CLUB, GREENPEACE, SAVE THE WHALES, SAVE THE REDWOODS, STOP GLOBAL WARMING and one that especially piqued my interest: PLF YES!

"What's this PLF button on your hat stand for, Mr. Stumple," I asked. "I'm not familiar with that one."

"Please call me O.B., all my friends do. Or Oddware. That was my mother's maiden name, you know."

"PLF. Yes, yes, of course. PLF stands for Plant Liberation

Front. We're a newly-formed focus group dedicated to the preservation of the earth's vegetation. Not just rain forests and trees, mind you, but everything that grows, down to even the most insignificant seedling. Everything has a purpose in the universe, you know. Everything is interrelated. Just because it is small and unpretentious doesn't mean that it's not important. PLF is working confidently — as we say in our mission statement — 'toward the day when all plant life will be free from abuse, neglect and exploitation.' A beautiful sentiment, don't you agree?"

Stumple stopped writing in his notebook and peered at me seriously. He blinked several times.

"Plants have feelings, too, you know. They cry out in pain, just as an animal does. If you know how to listen, you can hear their agony."

I thought I could see a tear forming behind the smudged glasses.

"It's an ecological crime that must be universally recognized sooner or later. PLF's mission is to spread the message far and wide until the peoples of the world realize the horrors they are unwittingly committing by the wonton destruction of vegetation. We will continue our program of education until we succeed, just as the fur lobby has, or the animal liberation army."

Stumple went back to his writing while I checked under my feet to see if I might have inadvertently stepped on a buttercup or something. My God, I thought. What I have encountered here goes way beyond your everyday fuzzy-brained environmentalist. If you will forgive

104

me for saying so Ralph, coping with talking bears is a cinch compared to fencing with a dedicated tree-hugger who had transferred his passion from old-growth timber and rain forests to the preservation of things like skunk cabbage and dandelions.

I sat down on the stump I had occupied during the earlier bear meeting and put my carton of empties on the ground beside me. Oddware was now sitting cross-legged on the ground, squinting at me through his foggy glasses with a look of anticipation. I could tell that he had been through this before and was preparing for an argument.

"Are you serious?" I inquired.

"Of course I'm serious," he replied, "and my supervising professor at Evergreen has agreed to allow me to investigate this for my doctorate. As soon as I have completed my present assignment, that is."

I was beginning to be mightily puzzled about which of the many things he had been talking about was his "present assignment," as he called it. "Tell me again what it is, I think I've forgotten. Something about washing machines, is that right?"

Oddware squinted and blinked rapidly. I had just slipped that washing machine business in there to see if I could get his goat but apparently he didn't have a goat. There was no reaction. This was a very serious young man, I concluded, showing the same kind of fervor you are likely to find among the "born-again" types of any persuasion.

"I'm just completing my survey of the biodiversity of our local environment," he went on. "Wildlife, insects, plant growth, the encroachment of human habitation, loss of animal habitat, that sort of thing. My interest in surreptitious garbage dumping has just grown out of my other studies.

"Would you like to look at my lists?" He began digging

through his backpack again.

"Sure," I said. Now here was something I can get my hands on, I thought. Garbage and junk. Forget the talking plants.

Out came another spiral notebook with "Listing of Illegal Dump Sites" written on the cover in bold letters. In smaller letters underneath I saw a bunch of section numbers and survey information. Stumple handed me the book from where he squatted on the ground.

"Now, if you look how I have arranged the material, you will see that I've noted the date, location as near as I could reckon it, and then a listing of actual items in the dump. And here I have a column for comments which includes any unusual characteristics." Stumple seemed pleased with his accomplishment.

Ralph's contribution to the environmental movement.

"I'm going to apply for a grant to have the college buy me a personal global positioner so that I can include the latitude and longitude of each dump and then my survey will be much more useful. You can readily see how one thing leads to another in my field. The inquiring mind of the true scientist is never at complete rest. I like to think that my interests are eclectic."

This is beyond eclectic, I thought. This is the scientific method turned on its head. I resolved to remain calm.

"You have a notation here: 'seven bullet holes.' What does that mean?" I asked, pointing to one of his entries.

"Well, you see," Oddware said, pointing with enthusiasm, "That's a fifty-gallon water tank that's been hit by gunfire seven times. Look at this one: 'GE dishwasher, fifteen large caliber holes.' There seems to be a kind of basic need of people to shoot at metal objects. The reason for this is not completely understood and I'm sure that our psychology people will want to add a study of this to their curriculum. When they do I know my data will become very valuable. This is the kind of serendipitous activity that excites the department heads and is the reason they like to have me out in the field so much."

I couldn't help thinking that if O.B. Stumple was on my payroll I'd want him out in the field as much as possible, too.

I checked my watch and realized that the time had gotten away from me. It was way past my lunch hour. I had been up there in the woods since early morning, but there were still far too many things I wanted to learn about my new friend to leave now.

"You don't look too comfortable there, Oddware," I observed. "Shall we find a better place to talk?"

"Not at all," he said. "I enjoy this position. I learned it years ago when I was a Boy Scout. You know, sitting around the campfire, telling stories, singing the old songs. The scouts got it from the pow-wows, drumming circles and potlatches of the Native Americans, of course. At Evergreen we often conduct our seminars this way. We think it brings us closer to the earth. Creates a closer bond, if you will, and a connectedness to the earth mother."

"Whatever," was about all I could think of to say. Makes for a mighty wet butt when it rains, I observed to myself.

"What other interesting classes have you taken at Evergreen?" I asked.

I knew they had some pretty far out stuff down there, Ralph, and I figured this was a good opportunity to see if the things you told me about the place were true. I remember you telling me that the place is "full of squirrels and weirdoes" as you put it, seeking to find the meaning of life by concentrated contemplation of their navels – a place built by fuzzy-brained politicians with too much money and too much time on their hands. Furthermore, you said they displaced a bunch of your relatives when they built the place which I agreed was unfortunate.

That story you told me about your cousin Octavia being run over by a bulldozer was very sad, Ralph, but I think it has left you with some serious biases about the place. Have you forgotten that they put up that nice memorial to your cousin with the little concrete meditation bench, dedicated to all who have "given their lives in the furtherance of educational programs that promote the protection of all living creatures?"

Beware of politicians with too much money.

I didn't tell Oddward any of this, of course. I didn't tell Oddware anything about you, Ralph. He would have thought I was crazy.

Then again, maybe he wouldn't.

All this stuff went through my mind before Oddware replied to my question about Evergreen's curriculum.

"Well, I'm sure you realize that TESC – that stands for our beloved 'The Evergreen State College' – gives students a great deal of latitude and since I had been to Harvard before I came west, they were sure that I had sufficient motivation, imagination and initiative to succeed in designing my own course of studies. Oh, I took some of their basic courses like 'Expression of Movement,' a delightfully evocative program where each student designs a dance to explain a concept, like the one I did in which I reveal the hidden connectedness between Geoffrey Chaucer's *Canterbury Tales* and the modern welfare state. Part of my dance required a movement done in the woods at night wearing only an athletic supporter, which I divested myself of as the dance progressed. Unfortunately, this was done during winter quarter when it was very cold. I took a chill, caught pneumonia and was not able to finish. Luckily my professor gave me full credit for 'daring initiative,' which he said was equally as important as finishing the entire performance as choreographed."

I feigned awe and interest, which took a certain amount of initiative in itself.

Oddware was warming to the subject and he proceeded to tell me about other courses including "Psychology of Dreams" (six credits), which is about what you would suppose it to be except you were required to have a dream and then analyze it. Oddware admitted that he was unable to produce a dream in spite of sleeping at every opportunity during the quarter and when he finally managed to have a short one toward the end of the course, he couldn't remember it. Once again the professor observed his diligence and dedication to the course requirements and awarded him full credit upon completion of a short paper on the reasons why he wasn't able to dream on command. It was done in the form of a "visually arresting illuminated manuscript."

"There were many others I could tell you about," Oddware explained breathlessly. "Sociolinguistics (four credits), was an exceptionally stimulating experience wherein we sat in an intimate circle on the classroom floor and spent the quarter talking about talking. It was enchanting!"

Oddware went on eagerly. "I discovered my real interest, though, was in a study of the outdoors. I am very close to having the course outline completed for my projected field of study, which I have tentatively called 'Woods in Crisis: The Sociological, Psychological and Political Implications of Dumping Illegal Refuse in Unlawful Places.' I'm working on the course description now. It will contain recommen-

dations to the state legislature and it will involve students in the political process to provide another dimension to the mix. Interconnectedness and interfacing are dynamics which must be an integral part of our examination of the problem."

My eyes were glazing over and I felt it necessary to change the subject. Clearly Oddware was prepared to go on, but I felt I was being drugged by sociolinguistic interconnectedness.

"So," I asked with some weariness, "how do you happen to find yourself in our modest little wilderness? You come from close-by?" I felt the need for a little "deep background," as the politicians say.

"Originally from the east, Vermont to be exact. Grew up in Boston. The Stumples go back a long time in New England." He picked up a small pebble and tested it with his tongue.

"You have acid soil here, did you know?" He made some notes on his clipboard. "I was accepted at Harvard, but discovered the regimen too confining. Even though it has a reputation for liberal thinking, I found the opposite to be true, at least so far as the science department is concerned. So, I quit Harvard and went to work for my brother Stemple."

"Your brother's name is Stemple?"

"Yes, curious, isn't it? My brother's name is Stemple O. Stumple. Bet you can't guess his middle name." Oddware gave a little giggle.

"My mother had a great sense of humor. She didn't have any male members left in her family and she was determined that the name Oddware not disappear from the New England social register, so she named my brother Stemple Oddware Stumple. Isn't that a good joke?"

"Delightful," I said dryly. "What kind of business is your brother in?"

"Stempie is in some kind of computer business, makes electronic things. I worked on his assembly line for a time, but I'm afraid my heart wasn't much in my work. I made a mistake and put a wrong part in whatever I was making which caused a big lawsuit because an insurance company lost all its computer records or something. Stempie suggested maybe I'd like to try a college out west some-where and said that he'd pay my way. He has oodles of money, you know. So I checked around and found The Evergreen State College. TESC, the 'Little Harvard of the West.' Liberal to a fault. We can design our own curricula – not even Harvard lets you do that. It's a beautiful concept and I've found a home here. You mind if I smoke?"

O.B. was fumbling around in his pockets and soon produced the "makin's," as we used to call them way back when I was a cowboy just learning to smoke. He rolled himself a small, skinny cigarette with that funny aromatic grass, twisted the end closed and set fire to the end of it with a big kitchen match. I'm not sure, but I think they call it a "toke" or a "doobie" or a "joint" or some such. I can't keep up with the new words kids make up nowadays.

"You like a drag?" he asked. "A little of this keeps your mind active. Does wonders for the creative juices."

"So I've heard," I said. "But I don't smoke anymore. The government says it's bad for me."

A cloud of odorous smoke formed around Stumple's head. I caught a strong whiff and for an instant thought maybe I had been hasty in turning down Oddware's offer. A bit of creative thinking might help in this situation.

"Did I tell you about the Essex?" Oddware asked.

"Eighty-seven bullet holes," I replied. "They weren't very good cars. I remember my uncle saying he wanted to shoot his. The damn thing would't back up. Had to keep it out on his farm 'cuz it took a half an acre to turn it around.

"You finding much wildlife around here?" I asked for want of anything else to talk about.

"Saw a red fox the other day."

"What was he doing?"

"The fox trot!" Oddware said, slapping his knee and cackling with such high-pitched glee that he set dogs to barking off in the distance.

112

"That's a good one, Odd," I said. "Fox trot, very good."

Doesn't take long for that stuff to take effect, I thought. I couldn't help wondering if you and Duffy were somewhere within earshot, Ralph. Your low opinion of the human race wasn't going to be improved any by the behavior of this unusual specimen.

Oddware's eyes seemed to be losing sharp focus, though in all honesty it was hard to tell through the smudgy spectacles. He had dug out his magnifier again and began studying what appeared to be an ant climbing up a stalk of grass.

"Here's your basic Red Ant. *Formica.* Lots of people call them piss ants. They're really not well-liked, you know. They bite when they're frightened or irritated."

Oddware blew a puff of smoke at the insect who immediately raced down the stalk, ran around in several circles in apparent confusion, then vanished into the forest undergrowth.

I couldn't help making an observation. "O.B., for one as sensitive to all creatures and plants as you seem to be, that appeared to me to be a decidedly insensitive act. The poor little creature is disturbed and upset."

I tried to sound like a truly concerned and compassionate fellow environmental-

113

ist, when in fact I've been known to stomp on ants with great glee, knowing full well that if the entire human population of the world were to stomp on piss ants until eternity we still wouldn't get rid of them all.

"Certainly not," replied Oddware, peering at me, blinking and smiling. "Those little fellows love the effect of *cannabis*. Did you see how quickly he ran away? He has headed straight to his nest to spread the word to the colony. Unless I miss my guess there will soon be hundreds of his friends over here seeking similar stimulation."

Oh, wonderful, I thought. Suppose some of them recognize me. I'll be bitten to death by a bazillion piss ants. A lot of the little bullies know of my animosity toward their kind.

Get hold of yourself, I thought. You're losing your grip. These aren't South American killer ants we're dealing with, and anyway, even in your pitiable physical condition, you can easily outrun a bunch of ants.

Just to be on the safe side I had Oddware make me one of his little homemade cigarettes so if the ant hordes arrived I would be able to pacify them with a bit of the soothing smoke. I congratulated myself on my cleverness and then, after I had taken a couple drags on the "joint" I promptly forgot all about the ants.

I don't remember too much about the rest of my visit with O.B. Stumple that afternoon. I think I must have "mellowed out," as they say. I recollect that I used the words "cool" and "awesome" a lot, and that we had a lengthy, and often spirited conversation about a range of subjects from the sad state of affairs in Tibet to the personalities of various kinds of vegetation. I distinctly remember him telling me that the human race is hurtling toward ultimate destruction and I resolved to remember to tell you this, Ralph. I knew you'd be pleased to hear it. Oddware showed me his membership card in a new environmental organization called E.S.I. which stands for "Earth Save International" whose stated goal is to "promote diet centered on fruits, vegetables, nuts, grains, and legumes for healthy living, provided we can harvest these crops in a humane way that does no harm to the plants."

"This will likely doom the root crop industry," I said. "But it will please the hell out of generations of children yet unborn, who will be spared having to sit at the dinner table far into the night, like I did when I was a kid, until they finish eating their turnips and beets."

Oddware ignored my jests and then said, with feeling, that furthermore, if pesticides are not curtailed, the earth was doomed. He blinked at me several times, awaiting my reply.

I remember telling him that if environmentalists weren't curtailed the same fate was equally assured.

Right then and there, I had inspiration for another quotation for the bear sign: "PITY THE BUGS FOR THEY SHALL INHERIT THE EARTH." I idly wondered if there were such things as environmentalist bugs. Probably wear thick, dirty little eyeglasses. Cool idea, I thought.

Talking to oneself is seldom profitable.

Oddware informed me several more times that humanity was doomed, but by then my head was beginning to hurt real bad, so I didn't much care.

The piss ants never did come back. Oddware said that they instinctively know when there's a *Homo sapiens* around who is prejudiced to their group.

So, the suspicion is that I'm bigoted, too.

Damn.

I had clearly lost track of time and the sun was glowing pink and orange in the western sky when I mentioned to O.B. that I hadn't had anything to eat since breakfast. He went rummaging around in his pack, sort of like Harpo Marx, and promptly came up with an environmentally-approved bar of nourishing nuts, fruits, grains and

legumes all humanely harvested by the E.S.I. people in a commune in Wisconsin. As I munched on this concoction, I read the label and was informed that everything in it was certifiably organic and that even the harmful bugs infesting the crops that the bar was made from were individually removed by hand by members of the commune and taken to a sanctuary where they were cared for until they could be safely released elsewhere.

I didn't mention it, but the thing tasted like tailings from a pulp mill.

Oddware had re-lit his roach which seemed to restore his cheerful demeanor. As we parted company, he said he sure hoped that he could find his VW bus, which he remembered leaving somewhere on Road 4432 not far from an unauthorized trash dump containing three old tires, a Sears Roebuck model 402 power mower (two bullet holes), and a bunch of rusty mufflers.

"I hope our paths will cross again," he said cheerily. "Here's my card. If you're ever near The Evergreen State College, look me up. They can most always tell you where to find me. Cheerio."

"Cool, man," I said.

Off he went, striding in his gangly way through the underbrush in an easterly direction, humming and trailing smoke, his golden ponytail – the student body emblem of TSEC – bobbing in the evening sunset.

I looked at his card. It took me a moment to get it into focus.

"Awesome," I said to myself.

When I got home I had a terrible headache and what sleep I got that night was troubled. I tried to convince myself that Oddware Stumple must have been a bad dream, but his calling card told me otherwise.

Well, there's the story Ralph. This unusual fellow drives the back roads in a Volkswagen camper with a chimney sticking out of the top. He's very friendly and perfectly harmless.

I'm sure he would be pleased to make your acquaintance.

ODDWARE B. STUMPLE
Naturalist
"In relentless search of truth"
SAVE MOTHER EARTH

CHAPTER EIGHT
Back to School

I didn't go back up the hill the next day even though I was still anxious to resolve the matter of the signs with Ralph and Macduff and to tell them about my adventures of the previous day. I had the uneasy feeling that some of that episode with Oddware Stumple had been witnessed by Ralph, at least, and probably by both of them. I wasn't particularly proud of my behavior, especially the part about smoking that pot, something I had never done before. For some reason I was worried about my "dignity." Old hang-ups die hard, I guess. Since when must one be dignified in front of a couple of wild bears, I asked myself? Jeez, perish the thought.

I went up the hill the following day to see if I could find my erstwhile friends and continue negotiations over the sign business. True to his word, Ralph was nowhere to be found.

"If the flag isn't in the stump, don't bother looking for me," he had said. "I won't be around."

When I reached the clearing where we had met two days before, however, I found what looked like a scrap of a soiled paper bag weighted down with a small rock. On the paper was crude writing done in brown crayon.

I read, "Wee falo odball beback sune. Duf."

This could only be a note from my bear friends written by young Duffy. It sort of answered the question about whether he could write, but didn't say much for his spelling. Well, it's a starting place, I thought. We can work it out.

I put the thing from my mind, or so I thought, and went about my business, part of which included coming up with original quotations for that burdensome bear sign.

One day, in apropos of nothing, I wrote a sign which read "NO PUBLIC RESTROOM HERE." The following day I was busying myself around my shop when a rather weary old car stopped, and a gaunt fellow in a suit and a tie got out. The first thing I noticed about him was that he was wearing a 16-inch collar around a 14-inch neck and his pants were about three inches too short. He was carrying a briefcase, and even though it was old and battered, a briefcase of any kind immediately puts me on my guard; it's an instinct I've never been able to outgrow. This guy was either a salesman or an evangelist. Lawyers don't usually carry scruffy, battered briefcases and they sure don't drive old cars. He asked me if people had been "misbehaving themselves" on the bear.

As I stood there mystified, he handed me one of those religious tracts that informed me that the "END OF THE WORLD IS NEAR" and suggested that since I had such a wonderful venue there on the side of the highway and such a wide audience of faithful readers, I should consider posting messages of a spiritual nature on the sign so that when the time came I might avoid the fate of so many of my

We were frequently annoyed by tourists.

fellow unrepentants who are doomed to roast forever in the nether regions of hell. He expressed his sincere assurance that I could avoid this unhappy fate if I were to provide more uplifting messages on the bear sign.

As a matter of fact, he had a booklet of just such messages, "used by all the major churches and temples," that he could let me have at a very reasonable price, as he put it. I supposed that he was concerned about my occasional intemperate jibes tweaking the "Born Again" set – such things as, "WHY IS THERE NO HUMOR IN THE BIBLE?" and "DON'T WORRY YOURSELF TO DEATH, LET THE CHURCH HELP." When he gave me a bunch of "Jesus Saves" stuff I couldn't resist the temptation to tell him that I had another great quote all ready to go. It says "JESUS SAVES, MOSES IN-

VESTS." Instead, I lied, saying that I had to get Ralph's permission before I could put uplifting messages on the sign. Male black bears are rarely into uplift of any kind, I said, and I would be jeopardizing my job if I was to go beyond my authorization.

He looked at me like maybe he didn't really want me on his side after all, and drove off talking to himself about the wages of sin, which reminded me that I had once put up a quotation that proclaimed that "THE WAGES OF SIN NEED NOT BE REPORTED," which, as we know, comes from the Internal Revenue Code.

A few mornings later, as I stood waiting for a break in the traffic so I could safely cross the highway to the shop, I glanced up the hill and saw that the flag was in the stump. Well good, I thought, perhaps now I can get the business about the signs resolved. I went back into the house and got the grubby piece of paper with its quaintly written note so I could show it to the bears. I  also intended to have a talk with Duffy about his spelling problems. At the last minute I thought to roll up a big old sketch pad that had been gathering dust in the corner of the shop and I stuffed a handful of crayons into my pocket, which I unrealistically thought might be useful if I made good on some kind of arrangement about getting the bears to write slogans for me. It wouldn't hurt to be prepared, I thought.

About halfway up the trail I realized that I hadn't brought along the Budweiser lubricant that I used to grease the more difficult aspects of our relationship. Well, tough luck, I said to myself, damned if I'm going back down now – it's too early in the morning for bears to be drinking, anyway.

When I got to the top there was no sign of Ralph or Duffy, but there was a large arrow scratched in the dirt pointing east in the direction Ralph had taken me once before when he told me all about his winter misfortunes. I wasn't keen about heading off into the wilderness, especially when it looked like it could start raining at any time, but I trudged on, taking careful note of landmarks so

I wouldn't lose my bearings going home. Soon I came to another small clearing where I saw a new arrow pointing north toward what appeared to be a barely recognizable trail into the huckleberry and manzanita bushes.

Way off to the southwest I could see one of the many power lines which run through our woods, giving me at least a general idea of where I was. I ventured a short distance in the direction indicated by the arrow and soon found myself going steeply downhill. I quickly began to think about turning around, knowing that every foot going down on the outbound trip meant an equal number of feet going up on the way home again. I felt the beginnings of impatience and agitation. Since when, I thought, did I have to chase these bears around in the middle of this tangled wilderness; if those inconsiderate beasts wanted to see me, by George, they could find a place convenient to me, not to them.

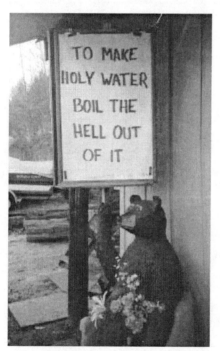

I found myself approaching a grove of large, old-growth fir trees set close together with a dense understory of cedar and hemlock. Suddenly I heard the unique popping sound that a black bear makes with its lips when it is warning of danger or is telling unwanted guests that they have come close enough. I stopped in my tracks, fervently hoping that this was my friend

Ralph talking and not one of his less friendly relatives.

With great relief I heard his voice call out, "It's okay, Macduff. It's the old man. Come on down."

And down a tree raced the little cub bear in a shower of bark and debris, all full of energy and excitement. He ran straight at me and I braced myself for a collision. At the last instant he veered off and commenced running around in circles like a puppy dog, beside himself with excitement. He then gave me a big hug around the knees.

To say I was touched would be an understatement. I patted him on the head, mightily pleased to think that someone in the bear world would actually show a sign of affection toward me. My pleasure was tempered, however, by the thought of those needle-sharp little claws only a denim's thickness from burying themselves into my leg.

"Come on along. Follow me," Ralph urged. "There's a better place to talk just ahead. We're too much out in the open here."

We proceeded down into a steep ravine and he seemed to be in a hurry to move on. Macduff continued to frolic, kicking up a flurry of forest litter.

"That'll do, Duffy," grumbled Ralph. "Never show too much affection to humans. When you do you can be labeled a 'nuisance' bear and, according to their rules, they then have the right to shoot you, or at the very least kidnap you and take you off into another county where they turn you loose among unfriendly strangers, which can be almost as bad."

By damn, I hadn't been in the old grump's company for more than a minute and he was already trying to start an argument.

"Dang it, Ralph, let the boy enjoy himself," I said. "I solemnly promise not to tell the authorities that I patted the little fellow on the head. Anyway, you're the one more likely to be labeled a nuisance. After all, it's you who's always rooting around in garbage cans, eating refuse, and stealing newspapers and dog food off back porches. I hope you're not teaching the cub to do that sort of thing."

Ralph looked at me with disgust. "This nuisance thing works both ways, you know. By the way, where's the beer? I thought we had an agreement about that."

"Yeah, our agreements have a way of going astray in both directions," I reminded him. "Anyway it's too early in the morning to be drinking beer. It's bad for your digestion. Furthermore, it's too heavy to carry way up here."

Ralph gets some of his stuff off bumper stickers.

"My God, listen to the excuses," grumbled the old bruin. "Before long you won't have to *carry* it up here anyway. You'll be able to drive it right up to my back door in full case lots. Did you know there was a bunch of surveyors down around our old berry patch the other day? I sneaked up close to them and gave a little snuffle. Put the fear of God in 'em and they took off running like scalded weasels. Left all their tools and papers lying right there on the ground and I got a good look at their charts."

"You know what they're doing?" He didn't wait for an answer.

"They're planning another one of those housing developments. Roads, curbs and gutters, fire plugs, the whole rigmarole. Going to call it 'Mountain Vista Estates, Affordable Luxury Living.' So, needless to say, if I'm going to stay alive much longer I'll probably have to move again. Now, you tell me who's the nuisance. Dammit, we bears were here first."

Ralph seemed genuinely depressed and I sought to cheer him up.

"These thing take a long while to develop, Ralph. You'll have plenty of time to find a new place."

I didn't feel nearly as hopeful as I tried to sound. Where could he go? Human civilization was closing in on bears and everything else. Well, this would have to be a problem for another day.

We had apparently arrived at our meeting place. Somehow I had the feeling that this little-used clearing in the deep woods on the side of a steep ravine must be very near Ralph's winter quarters which were probably in a cave or under an uprooted tree down near the bottom of the canyon where a small stream flowed. It was nicely hidden and secure from any casual traveler who might happen by. It seemed like the perfect spot.

Also, I remember him telling me a long time earlier, that he spent a lot of his daytime hours in a well-concealed treetop hideout. There were ample specimens of large old fir trees nearby that would serve the purpose admirably. I was also pretty sure that the land we were on was well outside the boundaries of the "Luxury Living" project and was part of the vast holdings of a large, well-known, local timber company. I tried to explain this to Ralph, but he didn't seem reassured. He knew as well as I that timber companies, large and small, are in the business of cutting down trees without much regard for how many bears or other creatures might live there.

We got ourselves settled down, as was our custom whenever we were about to enter into another episode of what I had come to call my "Conversations With A Bear" series. Ralph took a seat on an old stump while I perched on a log. Macduff jumped up and sat down by my side. The sky had begun to clear. The day was warming nicely, and I hoped that this session would be peaceful and pleasant without the distractions caused by beer bottles, rainfall or itinerant environmentalists. The setting seemed perfect for a civilized, well-reasoned conversation but, in light of the personality of the elder of my two companions, I had the feeling that this was likely to be too much to hope for. As I knew by now, bears can be difficult and today, in consideration of Ralph's depressed state of mind, it might be best if we avoided contentious subjects. Ralph was clearly preoccupied, his chin on his chest. Macduff fidgeted.

"Well, friends," I said. "You put up the flag. What's on the agenda?"

I thought I'd let the bears set the tone before I got back on the subject of the signs, which always seemed to lead to difficulties. I still had my tablet and crayons in my pocket.

"Jew get my note?" asked Duffy eagerly, peering into my face.

I feigned ignorance, thinking I might learn something more about my recent visitor, O. B. Stumple.

"The note I left back at the other place," he persisted. "After you talked to that man."

"He's talking about the note he left under a rock after you and your weird naturalist friend parted company," said Ralph wearily. "By the way, that was a rather disgraceful spectacle, if I do say so. Smoking pot is a young man's sport. Old geezers like you just look silly trying to look like hippies."

"So," I said with resignation. "I figured you were watching. Let's not make a big deal about it, shall we?"

"Mushrooms are better than that weed," Duffy chimed in. "I know where we can get some."

I knew I'd better get our conversation back on track lest we run afoul of our old focus problem again. I searched my pockets until I found the mystery note.

"Yes, I found your note, if that's what this thing is. Can you explain what it's supposed to say?"

"No problem, dude, it's easy." Duffy peered into my face. "Can't you read?" he asked seriously. Duffy took the crumpled scrap from my hand. Actually, he sort of speared the paper on one of his claws. "How come you can't read it? You want me to read it? That be cool?"

"That's cool," I said re-
signedly.

"Okay, look here," he
said eagerly, pointing at the
paper. "I'll teach you."

Ralph seemed disinter-
ested in the whole business.

Macduff went on, point-
ing to each scrawled letter
with his index "finger."

"The first word is 'we.'"

"The first letter in a sentence is always capitalized," I
said. "'We' has only one 'e.'"

Duffy rushed on, "'...are
faloing oddball.' That's that

127

goofy guy's name, 'member?"

"You left out the 'are' and following is spelled f-o-l-l-o-w-i-n-g. Oh, never mind," I said. "I think I get the message." I could see that Duffy was not paying a bit of attention to me.

"Then see, I signed my name. Duf. Reading is easy. I can teach you."

"Duffy has a small problem with dyslexia," grumbled Ralph.

"How can somebody with dyslexia read Shakespeare?" I asked him.

"With Shakespeare, dyslexia helps. Stuff doesn't make sense backward or forward anyway." Using his natural-born toothpicks, Ralph was trying to dislodge some-thing from his teeth.

Shakespeare is easy if you have dyslexia.

"OK, Duffy, let me see if I can read this by myself now. 'We are following Oddware, or Oddball as you call him, be back soon, signed Macduff,' is that right?"

"Yeah, dude, that's cool. I'll have you reading in no time."

"By the way, Duffy, it's 's-o-o-n,' not 's-u-n-e.' And 'be back' is two words, not one."

"Cool," was all Duffy could say.

He had found my writing tablet which I had laid on the ground and was showing signs of interest. "You got anything to write with, man? I'll practice my words."

I found the crayons and gave him one. He immediately fitted it backward between his two middle "fingers" so that he would write with his knuckles against the paper. He wedged the crayon in tightly; in large, lopsided letters he wrote his first words:

THIS IS CULE STUF DOOD.

I looked at Ralph who was scratching his belly, a bored look on his face.

"By George, Ralph," I said. "The boy shows promise. Phonetically speaking, at least, all we have to do is work on the spelling a bit."

"Mother taught us how to read and write but she never got around to spelling. She said English spelling was too stupid to bother with."

"By the way, Ralph, old buddy," I said pointedly, "the boy learned how to hold that crayon without a bit of trouble. How come you told me you couldn't do it?"

Ralph peered innocently up into a tree. "The younger generation picks up new technology quicker than we older folks," he said, without a hint of guile.

Damn, it was immediately clear that I had been hoodwinked again. There's something decidedly unsettling about being snookered by a bear.

"Your grandpa is a pettifogging old thimblerigger, Duffy," I said. "I should have learned long ago that there's nothing he won't do to avoid work."

"That's what grandma used to say, too," said the young bear idly drawing circles on the writing pad. "How do you spell that?" asked Macduff, his crayon poised.

"Spell what?" I asked.

"Pettyfoggingthimblerigger."

"S–n–e–a–k–y," I said. "D–e–v–i–o–u–s works, too."

Duffy began to write and soon ran off the edge of the page. "Forsooth, I need more room."

"Try smaller letters, and shorter words." I could see concentration building up on the little bear's face. This was a good sign. Just maybe we'll make a scribe out of the lad after all, I thought. "Hey, Duffy, see if you can think of a quotation for your grandpa's sign. Remember, it has to be short, now, not more than fifteen words."

I turned my attention to Ralph who was idly chewing on a piece of huckleberry bush.

"Well, Ralph, so you went off with Oddware. What did you learn? Does he really have an old Volkswagen?"

"Of course he has an old Volkswagen," Ralph grumbled, "with 'FREE TIBET' signs front and back. 'SAVE THE WHALES, SAVE THE TURTLES, SAVE THE OWLS.' Save everything. Everything except save the goddamned bears, that is. Why is it those tree huggers never consider saving bears?" Ralph seemed genuinely offended.

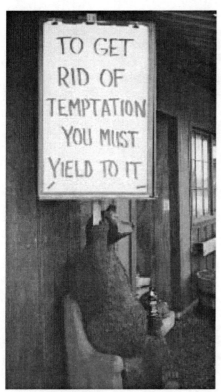

"I have a pretty good idea," I offered. "Bears are just plain too ornery. They don't appeal to sensitive people."

Ralph snorted.

"You know what grampa did?" Duffy asked me.

"No, Duffy, I'm almost afraid to ask. What did grandpa do?"

"He snuffled at Oddball. Tried to scare him."

"Did it work?" I asked.

"Hell no, it didn't work," grumped Ralph. "He just got out his notebook and began writing stuff down. Then he started taking pictures in all directions. He had no idea where we were. Even if he could see through those glasses, he would never have found us. Right, Duffy?"

"The guy's a nut case," said Duffy, looking up from his writing. "Takes great big steps and hums to himself all the time. He's hard to keep up with. He picked some of our mushrooms, too."

I was shocked. "He picked mushrooms?" I exclaimed. "That's against his religion. Did you hear the poor little things cry out?" I asked facetiously.

"No," said Duffy. "But he was talking to them."

"Did he say anything important?" I asked.

"Not unless you think apologizing to a mushroom is important," Ralph interjected, grumpily. "I hope he didn't plan to eat those things while he's smoking that dope. It's a bad combination. Shoot, he won't even need that old car. He'll just start flapping his arms like a damned old crow and fly all the way back to good old TESC. A guy like that full of psycho mushrooms and weed smoke is likely to attract a lot of attention, something we bears can do without. Anyway, we checked the other day and his old heap is gone so I guess we're rid of him. He's probably off somewhere else talking to bugs and counting holes in washtubs."

Ralph peered at me seriously. "You know, if there's a membership fee in the human race, I'd ask for my money back if I were you."

"Hey, Duffy," I said. "Get that one on your list."

"That's too many words," said Ralph, counting off on his fingers and toes. "That's nineteen."

"I'll fix it later," I said. I was elated. It seemed to me that we had suddenly worked out our whole problem. Accidentally and without rancor, argument or bloodshed.

I looked at Duffy. He was lying on his stomach chewing his

tongue with his brow knitted in intense concentration, writing "IF THERS MEMBER SHIP IN HUM RACE GET MUNNY BAK IF IU." I might need a translator, I thought, but it was a start.

"Here's another one, Duffy." said Ralph. "MILLIONS FOR OWLS NOT ONE CENT FOR BEARS. HOW COME?"

"I used that one a long time ago, Ralph," I said.

"Doesn't hurt to say it again. Say it every week would be about right. Keep the issue before the public where it should be." Ralph had started to his feet which is a bad sign. It signified agitation which I was determined to avoid.

"We don't want to lose our readership," I said. "Too much repetition is not good. Keep the messages fresh and timely. That way your audience will stay interested."

"My God," grumbled the old bear, settling back to his seat. "Sounds like we're selling soap."

"Try to remember, Ralph, that I've been doing these signs all by myself for a long time," I said, "and I pride myself on the fact that I haven't repeated myself yet. Now that we've found out that Duffy can write the signs, I expect you guys to come up with some original stuff. We can jazz up this whole operation."

"Yeah, sure," said Ralph without much interest. "You and Duffy work it out. I got other things on my mind. Like where I'm going to move to when those damnable developers get started on their luxury estates. Luxury estates, that's a good one, probably be just a bunch of trailer houses."

"Each one will mean another garbage can," I said, trying to inject something positive into the conversation.

"Not to mention more dogs," Ralph snorted. "You know, if dogs were smart enough to talk they wouldn't be man's best friend very long."

"Hey, get that down, too, Duffy." I looked around and Duffy wasn't with us. "Where's the cub gone, Ralph?" I asked.

"Probably lost interest in this sparkling conversation," grumped the old bear. "He's a whole lot smarter than a dog."

I began to search around beyond our little clearing.

"Don't worry, he'll be back. His stuff is still here," said Ralph pointing to the paper and crayons. "You've got him all revved up about this writing gig. He'll be making your signs 'till you're sick and tired of the whole thing."

What do tree huggers have against bears?

"Don't forget now, you've got to help him. This statue and sign business was mostly your idea in the first place. Don't make the boy do all the work. No more weaseling, Ralph." I tried to make myself sound tough and forceful which I knew was a waste of effort..

Duffy reappeared dragging what appeared to be a small box at the end of a rope which he had in his mouth. "I just remembered this thing I found the other day," he said dropping the "rope," which was actually an electrical cord connected at the other end to a laptop computer. It was somewhat the worse for wear from having been dragged through the dirt. "It's got numbers and letters on the top. Looks like the whole alphabet. Can we use it?" he asked eagerly.

"Good grief, where did you get that?" I asked.

"Those surveyor people left it behind when they ran off," said Duffy. "I brought it home and Grampa said I could keep it. He said it's a commuter and you can write things with it but he doesn't know how to work it. Do you? Can you show me?" he asked eagerly.

I looked over at Ralph, who was pretending to be asleep.

"Ralph," I said. "This is a very expensive piece of high-tech hardware that you've stolen from those people. You could be charged with felony theft here."

"Big deal," said Ralph with disgust. "Those people can be charged with expropriation of private property without just compensation which, I believe, is forbidden by your damned constitution. Let's call it an even trade."

"Heaven helps those who help themselves," said Duffy brightly. "Shall I write that on the list?"

"No," I said. "That one is just a bit too old, Duffy. Let's have a look at your machine. By the way, it's a computer, not a commuter, and it does write words and a whole lot of other things, too."

"Cool, let's make it go."

I opened the cover and blew out the dust. It wasn't too badly soiled. When I hit the "on" button it fired right up and the battery seemed to be fully charged. I opened up a document and the words "MOUNTAIN VIEW ESTATES PRELIMINARY FIELD NOTES" appeared, followed by several pages of numbers and figures. Hieroglyphics left by the surveyors, no doubt. I found the word processor and typed a few words. Duffy was beside himself with excitement.

"Hey Grampa, look! It makes words! All you've got to do is

poke the letters. Come look, Gramps, this is cool! We can make the signs on it."

Ralph was doing his best to show disdain. "I've heard about those modern gadgets, and frankly I have no interest in them. They're designed by madmen to confuse the rest of us. I don't plan to encourage them.

"Think of the paper we'll save, Grampa."

"Oh, good grief," groused the old bear. "Not that old argument again. Mark my words, Duffy, you get started on one of those things, you're going to forget how to be a bear. The same thing happened to your cousin Hotspur over in Oakdale. He got so wound up playing games on a computer he forgot to watch out for the wardens. They caught him in a net and now he lives in a zoo down in Tacoma. Sits in a cage all day drooling. People pay money to watch him through a fence."

Ralph got up slowly and shuffled down the hill. "I'm going to take a nap," he said over his shoulder. "I didn't get much sleep last night. You do what you want. All this thinking makes my head hurt." He disappeared through the huckleberry thicket. "Remember Hotspur, boy. Don't let it happen to you."

"Your Grandpa is not in very good humor today, Duffy. He's worried about what's happening to his territory. We've got to try to cheer him up. By the way, what's a Hotspur?" I asked.

"Hotspur is a character from Shakespeare's *Henry the Fourth* – a self-important blatherskite. Nobody important. I don't even know what bear he's talking about. One of his Kamilche cousins, I guess. Come on, let's work the commuter."

So for the next hour we did work the computer. I explained to the young bear what little I know about writing with the thing, but we found out he couldn't hit just one letter at a time, what with the way his claws were arranged, so we resorted to him punching each key with a stick. I couldn't locate a spell checker on the machine so Duffy went on happily misspelling almost every word. No matter – even a spell checker wouldn't have been able to decipher what word he was trying to write.

Duffy even thought up a couple of quotations all by himself: "IF AT FYRST U DON'T SUCEDE U R ABOT AVRAGE" and "A BARE IN HES TYME PLAYS MENNY PRTS." I fixed the spelling, but I could see that this could turn into a full-time job. It might be quicker to just write the signs by myself, I thought, but I decided to let the youngster stumble along and I would do what I could to keep things straightened out.

We spent the rest of the afternoon fiddling with the computer until he became quite proficient at poking the keys and getting sentences put together even though no progress was made with the spelling.

With a 'commuter,' we can save lots of paper.

Since there was no printer with the computer, we decided that Duffy would carry the machine down to the big stump and put up the flag when he thought he had a number of good quotations. Then I would retrieve the computer, plug it into my printer, and print up the list. After charging the battery I would return it to the stump for him to pick up. I tied the electrical cord in a loop so he could hang the computer around his neck instead of dragging it through the dirt and promised him that I would fix a box to put the computer in when he brought it down to the stump so it wouldn't get wet. I explained to him that he had to keep it out of the rain and that he mustn't allow it to get dirty because it was a delicate instrument and very expensive to repair. I couldn't take it anywhere for repairs anyway because they would find out it was stolen and I would go to jail.

I knew the whole thing was a ponderous arrangement and I began to think that it would probably be easier to let Duffy write the stuff on paper as we had originally intended. Not the least of my turmoil was the nagging problem that I was doing all this with a stolen computer. I had a mental picture of me standing handcuffed in front of a judge whining, "But you honor, I was only doing this so Duffy, the cub bear could write signs for his grandfather's statue."

Ralph hadn't returned by the time I headed back home. I told Duffy to have his grandfather put up the flag for me if he learned anything new about the "Vista Estates" project.

On the way back down the hill I realized that I had learned the answer to two questions, one of which had been puzzling me since I first met Ralph several years earlier. I now knew the location of Ralph's living quarters. When Duffy had left to get the computer he had only been gone for a few minutes, which meant that their home was probably only a short distance away. It was, as I suspected, down in that canyon, which I came to refer to as 'Bear Gulch." It wasn't very original, but quite accurate.

Secondly, I had an explanation to a mystifying article I had seen in the local paper just a few days earlier. I looked it up again when I got home. On the page where the police reports from the previous week were listed was the following:

"A member of the surveying crew working on a development near Highway 106 reported the theft of a laptop computer on Tuesday afternoon. He said his crew was surprised by two thieves who appeared suddenly out of a thicket of underbrush. They were described as a man and a boy in elaborate disguises which resembled Halloween costumes. The man carried a large automatic pistol and spoke in a guttural voice. Valuable information is stored in the computer, the worker said, and the loss of the data will result in a considerable delay in finishing the project.

"Police say they have no suspects. An investigation is continuing."

As I sat around the house that evening I tried to list the growing number of complications that had come into my life since I had made the acquaintance of that roguish old bruin. Now, I would have to add "felon in possession of stolen property" to the list.

I slept restlessly.

CHAPTER NINE
Ah, what tangled words we weave

It was much longer than I expected before I heard anything from young Duffy. I had really thought that his excitement about the computer would have resulted in an immediate response in the form of long lists of misspelled quotations for me to unravel and translate into usable English. Such was not to be. I had to go on as usual, finding my own whimsies wherever I could, doing my best to be original and creative. True enough, it was late fall and with winter coming on there was the possibility that the bears were heading underground, but I couldn't believe that Macduff was going to go off and leave me in the lurch after we had spent so much time discussing his responsibility in the quotation project. Ralph was capable of such behavior, but Duffy struck me as a thoroughly trustworthy little fellow who wouldn't let me down without giving me reasons why.

Weeks went by and I knew that the battery in the laptop must have long since gone dead. I became apprehensive. Had the surveyors returned with guns? Was the sheriff patrolling the backwoods looking for computer thieves? There was little I could do to relieve my anxiety but wait and watch for the flag in the stump. More time went by and it wasn't until a rainy Monday morning in late November that the signal appeared.

I hoped that the computer was in the box I had provided and that I wouldn't have to go clear up the hill in search of the bears. Even though I was keeping the trail in good repair, I found that the force of gravity seemed to increase, year by year, and climbing that hill was becoming less and less appealing. I bundled up in my rain gear and set off up the grade.

The computer was in the box and it seemed to be in good shape. So far so good. I returned to the house, plugged in the machine, punched up the word processor and hoped for the best. Words came up, lots of them. Actually, at first glance, they looked more like letters than words. I hooked up the printer and pushed the button. Thirty-eight pages came out – thirty-eight pages that seemed likely to keep me at my cryptology desk for most of the rest of the winter.

To my relief, at about page seven, Duffy apparently found the spell checker feature on the computer. Things got easier, but only relatively so, since spell checkers do nothing about convoluted syntax and muddled thinking. For the first four pages Duffy used no periods or capitals and, most aggravatingly, not even any spaces between his "words." As an example, I will transcribe a paragraph or two from page one, which I remember took me at least a day to untangle. I really don't know why I even decided to try.

IgettheCwurkinpreetygudbuticentseinkaveit2derkimuppintre&
sumtymitsrayn7ihev2queetrgonwayluk4nooplac2liv

The first thing I had to do was separate the words. It took a while but I finally got it:

i / get / the / C / wurkin / preety / gud / but / i / cent / se / in / kave / it / 2/ derk / im / upp / in / tre / & / sumtym / its / rayn / & / I / heve / 2 / queet / r / gon / way / luk / 4 / noo / plac / 2/ liv

From here on it was pretty simple, but his first message was not very informative:

hayluk I cn wryte wrds!

"I got the computer working pretty good but I can't see in the cave. It's too dark. I'm up in (the) tree and sometimes it rains, and I have to quit."

I decided that "r" stood for "Ralph" so the message went on to read: "Ralph (has) gone away looking for (a) new place to live."

That last bit was something of a surprise. I thought Ralph would get over his funk and wait awhile to see what events might transpire on the "development" project before he decided to leave the area. From all I had read about bears, they move only reluctantly from an established territory.

The next several pages were pretty much in the same vein – typical juvenile stuff about the weather, huckleberries, ants and mushrooms. I got so I could sort of scan a page of "Duffy's disorder," as I came to call it, and tell whether it was worth the effort of trying to decipher it.

This entry turned up on page four and appeared to have information of interest:

"onuvmicuznnemdclaudiofrumdoneer

gulphcorssedhesorrweetnicluklidybare

hangnrnd gulphcorsatnigtduin 'zigzig' atniteweytugor!"

Untangling this little gem took the better part of two days, but it was worth it. I won't burden the reader with the tedious steps involved, but I swear, this is what it said:

"One of my cousins named Claudio (that's another Shakesbear, of course) from down near (the) gulf coarse said he saw Ralph with (a) nice looking lady bear hanging around the gulf coarse doing "zig zig" at night. Way to go, Grampa!"

I made a note to ask Ralph about "ziz zig" the next time I saw him. If it was what I suspected it was, it seemed rather late in the year for such activities, but then I don't know everything about bears.

Ralph must have come home about the same time Duffy found the spell checker on the computer and probably told the cub to get busy on the project of writing quotations for the sign. The next dozen pages contained columns of witticisms both useful and not. Miraculously, the words began to be separated by spaces, which was a great improvement, and I was sure that Ralph had a hand in that as well. Here are a few samples of Ralph's and Duffy's early efforts:

- *It's better to have loafed and lost than never to have loafed at all.*
- *Black bear seeks companion. No dogs need apply.*
- *When a dollar was worth a dollar I didn't have a dime.*
- *A political speech is like archery. Allow for the wind.*
- *Limitations of space restrict my pronouncements here.*
- *Movies have gone from silent to unspeakable.*
- *Don't take to crime. There are lots of legal ways to be a crook.*
- *Bears are not covered by plagiarism or copyright laws.*
- *Be thankful we don't get all the government we pay for.*

- *I seek lodgings free from fleas and bugs if possible.*

- *A lawyer is a man who seeks to get what's coming to him.*

- *This is too much to bear (when Ralph was a cub he thought Tumuchtubear was his name).*

- *Unless I get a raise here I may GLUNCH (look it up).*

- *My God! The government says bear meat must be thoroughly cooked.*

- *We need straight talk about gays.*

- *How come there's no horse manure in Western movies?*

- *"Basically" is now the word of choice. It replaces "ya know."*

I think this gives you an idea about the intellectual level of our efforts. Ralph often gets steamed up about some political outrage or another and rails constantly about the treatment of bears and the stupidity of the human race. He chewed me out one time when he thought one of the signs I put up was too sentimental.

"Dammit," he said. "Don't put that kind of stuff on my sign. Leave that sloppy stuff to the churches. I'm a bear and I will speak like a bear. I have a reputation to uphold. Misanthropy is my birthright!" He

Sometimes I have to get Shakespeare out to look up Duffy's quotations.

143

thumped his chest like a gorilla, growled ferociously and stomped around, posturing. At the time I was frightened and started to run for cover, but that was before I knew that this kind of behavior was mostly just bluster. Still, I tried to keep the signs reasonably curmudgeonly in keeping with his cranky character. It made our friendship much easier to maintain and it did no harm except for the occasional criticism I got from some of my more delicate readers.

Then another undated message from Duffy turned up on page fifteen.

"I think commuter battery run down sew I went down 2 old man Pistoff place and plugged in to he elect out lit in he chick in house it charged up good all okaydokay now."

What Duffy was telling me was that he had taken the "com-

muter" down to the dumpy shack of a guy the bears had nicknamed "A.J. Pistoff" and had plugged it into an outlet in his chicken house and charged it up. The old guy's name was actually Armando J. Piskerof, but Ralph thought Pistoff fit him better because he was always mad and constantly yelling at something – his wife, his dog, his old car, brushpickers, goddamned rain, mud holes and on and on.

It's hard to figure how Duffy got in and out of the place without catching a load of buckshot. He probably slipped in while A..J. and his wife

Emmer were off to town in their '65 Buick "buyin' vittles and chickenfeed."

It seemed that Duffy had made friends with Pistoff's old lazy dog and pretty much had the run of the place when the old man wasn't home. Duffy made sure he never messed with the chickens, although he did get into the garbage can now and then in a neat sort of way, not that there was much in there to choose from. He and the dog shared what he found. The dog's real name was "Piskerof's Pride of Wilderness Valley" and he supposedly had papers and everything, but according to Duffy old Pistoff never called him anything except "You God Damned Worthless Old Mutt."

After the entry about recharging the battery there followed many pages of new quotations, some of which I had seen before and sometimes in exactly the same order. I soon realized that Duffy had learned how to access the Internet and had stumbled upon a gold mine of quotes, quips, wisecracks and homilies. Endless numbers of them. The source of the stuff didn't matter so much, I guess, just so I didn't have to think it up myself. I wasn't going to be able to tell my critics that these quotations were all original any more, not that I cared much. All but the most naïve didn't believe me, anyway.

I was just a bit piqued to think that that old reprobate Ralph had snookered me again. He had set me up in this enterprise and for years – yes, years – he had let me struggle with finding "funny" things to put on the signboard. Then after our big confrontation to get that responsibility straightened out he gets his innocent little grandson, who is even willing to learn to type in order to do it, to take over the job. Finally he arranges to steal a computer, has the kid learn how to use it, and then finds the stuff he needs already written, digested, time-tested and served up free-of-charge on the Internet. As all these thoughts passed through my mind, I pictured Ralph sitting up there on the hill, cross-legged on a stump – totally pleased with himself, smirking and eating huckleberries while purple slobber dripped from his lips.

Ralph seldom passed up an opportunity to proclaim the superiority of bears over people. (I don't always correct his spelling.)

Could it be that this damned old bear was smarter than me?

CHAPTER TEN
The Winds Of Change

With winter coming, I thought it best to get the computer back to Duffy before he went off to hibernate if such was his plan. I charged up the battery and returned the machine to the rendezvous point where I raised the flag and went back to the house to examine the rest of the thirty-seven pages that I had printed out.

Duffy, I discovered, had taken literary flight, and was soaring well beyond his assigned task of writing mere quips and quotes. He had begun experimenting with his new-found medium and on each page he astonished me with some new item of linguistic quirkiness. I still had to correct a lot of mistakes, but he was getting better. For instance, on page eighteen, in the midst of a lot of doodling, was the following limerick:

> *"There sits this old bare in a chare*
> *hoo thinks things in life are unfare*
> *So he vents all his gripes*
> *In curmudgeonly swipes*
> *On a sign that he holds in the are."*

"That's dedicated to Grampa," he wrote.

Following this entry, in apropos of nothing, came a well-known quotation from Dorothy Parker or Oscar Levant or somebody:

> *"The only thing worse than being misquoted is*
> *not being quoted at all."*

This was followed by a string of the less familiar, including:

"What's a politician mean when he says
    'We must take back the future for our kids???"
"Does an individual have a rite to assemble with himself??"
"What is a middlesex? Am I one??"
"I think I have cum down with IAD witch stands for
    Internet Addiction Disorder."
"Grampa has AADD witch is Adult Attention Disfunctional
    Disorder. He has gone off down to the gulf coarse again. I told him
    that he is putting himself in harms way. The old goat needs
    adult supervision."
"Growing old is mandatory – growing up is optional."

This sort of babble went on for page after page and I quickly came to the conclusion that Duffy was reading too many newspapers or spending way too much time on the Internet.

On page twenty-six, there appeared two more poems (at least I assumed they were poems):

> *"The wet black snout explored the forest floor*
> *lifting the leeves*
> *The truffles had left no sine of having bin there*
> *So he sougt the next best variety and watched the old*
> *Fishermans boot struggle to negotiate the small waterway*
> *Burdened by the hindering stones*
> *Nearby the nuthatch sounded its upside-down warning.*
> *He new there must be an old fisherman nearby in one boot."*

> *"I am trying to find my muse."*

Then:

ODE TO THE COMMON SLUG

(I fixed the spelling on this one although I'm not sure it helped much).

> *"Thou slimy bride of silence*
> *Thou still and wetted sloth*
> *What frond fringed legend haunts thy shape*
> *Your pipes and trimbles speak of nothing*
> *What mutes your struggle to escape.*
> *Slide aside my ugly friend, keep moving on your way*
> *I have no time to bide with thee I dare not waste my day."*

"HELP STAMP OUT SLUG SLYME"

It was clear to me that Duffy had been into his *psilocybin* mushroom patch again and had overdosed.

Reading his work brought to mind a quotation of T.S. Eliot (who didn't always follow his own advice):

> *"In the case of many poets, the most important thing for them to do ... is to write as little as possible."*

"BEAR THE BURDEN BUT DO NOT BURDEN THE BEAR"

> *"Did you hear the one about the kid who went out on Halloween dressed as a horse but the guy who was going to be the back end of the horse didn't show up so he went trik or treating all over town dragging his ass behind him?? HA HA I made that up miself."*

> *"Why do they call it a bare market? Do they sell bares there?"*

*   *   *   *   *   *   *   *   *   *   *   *   *   *   *   *   *   *   *

Several days passed and I was still trying to digest all this stuff when I noticed the signal in the stump. What now, I wondered? I truly hoped there was not another huge batch of nonsense on the computer. It was going to take weeks to sort out the stuff I already had. I needn't have worried. The only thing in the box was a scrawled note written on some of the paper I had given Duffy weeks before:

"Grampa hasnt come back, I don't know where he is maybee the gulf coarse but it is getting cold and I am tyred I am going to take a napp DUFF."

I was glad for the respite after that autumn of intense activity. It seemed that I was spending way too much time tending to bear matters and not nearly enough on my own. I had plenty of Duffy's quotations to last me through the winter, but just to make sure, I stopped changing the signs every other day and went to a three-day interval. I don't think anybody even noticed the difference.

We had several snowstorms that winter and a long spell of very cold weather. I couldn't help but wonder how my friends were coping. Bears survive very well in even the worst conditions as long as they are secure in their winter quarters, but I remembered that the last message I had from Duffy reported that old Ralph had gone off somewhere. God knows where. Well, by George, that grouchy old bruin had survived plenty of years without any help from me and I suspected he would continue to do so. Nevertheless, there was still that small twinge of worry.

I heard nothing from the bears until spring. It was late March, to be exact, on what was one of the first warm days of the year, when the signal flag appeared again. By now the old rag had become tattered and faded so I took along a piece of bright red cloth as a replacement. I thought it likely that there was just a message for me in the box, so I didn't go up the trail with the idea that I would be making that wearyingly long hike to the bears' hideout. Sure enough, there was a message. No computer, just a sheet of paper, sloppily folded, with puncture marks in it as though Duffy had carried it in his mouth. It was written in the young bear's scrawl, this time in blue crayon, and it showed no great improvement in legibility or spelling:

> *"R came back verry skinny he is stil asleep there is trubble up hear*
> *Menn working on rodes come on Sunday wenn wkrs are gon I*
> *will wake up R comuter is broke DUFF"*

So, the inevitable "march of civilization" was closing in on my friends and at a much faster pace than I had anticipated. To be sure, for some weeks I had been hearing the occasional rumblings of heavy machinery off in the distance, but had attached no particular importance to how it might relate to the well-being of my hibernating friends. Quite honestly, I hadn't been thinking about bears at all since the end of our last cold spell in early February. I still had plenty of quotations and naturally assumed that Duffy would show up with a new batch soon enough.

the comuter is broke sory.

The information that the "commuter was broke" was a minor distraction. More ominous was Duffy's disclosure of men building "rodes." I made plans to pay my friends a visit, but decided that I should undertake a scouting mission first.

So the very next day I set off in the old pickup to see what I could see. To get even close to the bears' winter quarters by vehicle I had to drive completely through the "new" development (which was hardly new anymore, having been there for at least fifteen years), out the dirt road past old Edna Harnessup's stump farm and down to the power line along a potholed series of deep ruts. I negotiated some scary waterholes whose depths could not be easily determined from the driver's seat and eventually came to the end of the road which was still at least a mile from the place where I had last visited Ralph and Duffy the previous year. Since there was no sign of new "rodes" I retraced my route. When I reached old widow Harnessup's place she was outside feeding her flock of scrawny chickens. She waved me a greeting so I stopped to chat.

"Howdy, Edna," I called. "How's it going?"

"Oh, can't complain too much," said the wispy old recluse. "Dang glad winter is over. 'Bout had enough of cuttin' firewood." She flung a handful of scratch to the squawking chickens.

Edna was sort of a "Ma Kettle" character who had lived alone out there in semi-isolation on five acres of gravel since that day several years earlier when her late husband Cutler, an emigrant from eastern Kentucky, had carried a half case of dynamite out into the woods, sat down on it and touched it off. Suicide was strongly suspected but, except for his hat which was lodged in a branch half way up a tall fir tree, there was never enough evidence left to prove anything one way or another. Cutler always had trouble holding jobs and acquaintances said Edna used to nag him constantly about this failing. "Damned old fool couldn't even grow marijuana way out here in the sticks without gettin' caught," she would complain. "Dumber than a pile of used hay wire he was."

Edna came over to the door of the truck and I could see that she'd been growing whiskers since the last time I saw her.

"Edna, you know anything about new roads being built around here?" I inquired.

"God spare us, I hope not," she said. "Got too danged many roads around here now. Kid came through here 'tother day on one of them scooter bikes. Had his hat on backwards, goin' lickety cut. Dang near run over old Wellington." Wellington was Edna's yellow cat who liked to sun himself on the dirt road in front of the old lady's shack.

"I'm thinkin' of puttin' up a gate out here. Slow 'em down a little, maybe. You can easy tell the young 'uns who are the hoodlums. They always got their hats on backward."

"Hey, Edna, you ever see any signs of bear around here?" I asked, thinking it would be interesting to know if my friends hung around in this area.

"Seen a big 'un just goin' into them woods over there last fall," said Edna, pointing off in the direction of the power lines. "He stopped and

Ralph still seeks companionship.

looked at me for quite a spell, then just sorta' shuffled off into them trees. I kept my shotgun handy, thinkin' he might come back. Fraid he might try to get at my chickens. But I ain't gonna' bother him if he don't bother me."

"Those old black bears are more likely to get into your garbage can than to bother your chickens," I said. "Just be sure you keep the lids on tight." I eased the truck into gear.

"Well, it's good to see you again, Edna. Gotta keep moving; see about those new roads. Take care of yourself."

"Don't hardly make no garbage. Anyways, I put a bungee cord across the top. Bears can't figure out a bungee cord," Edna said as I drove off.

Well, *most* bears can't, I thought to myself.

I went back into the development and then made a right turn off toward the east, down Christmas Tree Road, as they call it, which took me a considerable distance to the northern boundary of the settlement. There the blacktop ended and an old logging road took over. I knew I must be somewhere near that old blackberry patch where Ralph and I had first met so long ago. The patch had long since ceased to be and the berries had migrated off to a new location. Soon, I could see signs of recent logging; most of the larger trees had been cut and hauled away and the old logging roads had been turned into new logging roads. It became clear that Duffy was right — new roads were indeed being built. I was sure that I couldn't be more than a mile from Ralph and Duffy's winter quarters, but rather than run afoul of loggers and road builders, I retraced my tracks and went home. I would return on Sunday when the workers were absent.

I remembered to lay in a supply of cheap beer which I planned to use to loosen Ralph's tongue just in case he might be in one of his non-communicative funks. Then, as so often happens, a downpour of rain began on Saturday and continued right on through Wednesday. I knew that the road builders probably wouldn't be working, but certain that I would get stuck in the mud if I attempted to drive up there, I left a note in the message box for Macduff telling him I would try to make it up the following Sunday. On the next Sunday it was raining again, so I took another note up to the box and found one there for me:

> *"Yu betr cum sune. The watr is a raisen in the crik and R's viry upsett says hes goin leeve. He jest wok up and hes maddern hek I think he mite atack werkrs. DUFF"*

I scribbled a new note to Duffy telling him to try to get Ralph calmed down and that I would be up the next Sunday, rain or shine. As it turned out, Sunday started off as a nice day so I set off early, nervous as could be, hardly knowing what to expect. It had been more than half a year since Ralph and I had last met and I had the uneasy feeling that his disposition - usually just grumpy and disagreeable - might be turning hostile. When I got to the construction area I found that the workers had spread gravel on the roads. They were rough but

passable. Now all I had to do was try to find where the bears were.

Everything looked different. Big trees were gone and the underbrush was all trampled down. Piles of dirt were everywhere along with ditches and pipes. My God, even fireplugs! Small wonder the bears were nervous! This part of their homeland, where generations of Shakesbears had lived and died, was being forever changed. As had happened so many times in the history of America, the natives were being kicked off their land. I almost hoped I wouldn't be able to find Ralph; I knew he was going to be "mightily pissed," to put the matter in modern terminology. I tried to think up a variety of rationalizations to soothe what I suspected were going to be eruptions of ursine displeasure.

Off toward the east the terrain canted steeply downward and in the distance I could see a copse of misshapen old-growth trees that had a familiar look. That big one in the middle with the flattened top, I said to myself, is the summer hideaway of my friend Ralph, the misused *Ursus americanus*, and somewhere just beyond and below the tree is his underground winter home.

I parked my truck, hefted my backpack, which I had loaded that morning with four large salami sandwiches and two six-packs of oversized, long-necked bottles of cheap beer, and feeling a bit like Stanley setting out to find Dr. Livingstone, headed off into the underbrush toward the distant "Bear Gulch."

I felt surrounded by an invisible aura of sacrifice and martyrdom, venturing fearlessly into the unknown to assist old friends in their hour of travail and need. Well, that's what I thought, anyway.

Heading off into the underbrush toward the distant "Bear Gulch."

CHAPTER ELEVEN
Sea of Troubles

I had never been down into that deep canyon before. My only previous visit to the place was during my last conversation with the bears when I had spent the entire time up on the top of the hill trying to show Duffy how to run that purloined laptop computer.

"Bear Gulch" was a dark, gloomy place, reached by traversing a steep, slippery hillside which was even more treacherous than my own hill and without the benefit of the switchback trail. All this was made even more difficult by the several inches of rain we had experienced the last couple of weeks. I descended with trepidation, hanging onto every available hand-hold, part of the time on my feet but mostly sliding on my backside, gathering mud as I went. For a variety of reasons, I was unusually apprehensive about this visit to the bears.

First of all, this was a forbiddingly dark canyon, anything but inviting. I knew that Ralph had always been extremely secretive about the location of his lair, and as well as I knew him by this time, I still couldn't be certain that he was going to welcome me into this confidence. Down in the bottom of the canyon, I could hear the water rushing through the depths as the rains had brought a flood to what was normally a mere trickle.

I was quite sure that this is where the bears lived, but my next problem was how to let them know that I was in the vicinity. Yelling didn't seem like a good idea lest I attract unwanted attention. Shouting out in the woods is usually a sign that somebody is in distress, which I wasn't. Not yet anyway. I thought about whistling except that I had recently discovered that I had lost the ability to whistle. Somebody told me that this often happens to old geezers like me - something goes wrong with the pucker; I put this down on my list of things to worry about at some other time. At the moment, I didn't even know which way to go - upstream or down - and the rush of water in the creek was going to make it difficult to be heard over the racket.

Then I had a brilliant idea. Suppose I just open one of my bottles of beer and spill a bit of it on the ground? Bears have a keen sense of smell so Ralph would surely pick up the scent and he would find *me* rather than vice-versa. I removed my backpack and dug out a bottle.

As I began to twist off the cap, I was startled by the sound of an object striking the ground behind me, and turning, I discovered a small, badly used and well-worn book half imbedded in the mud a few feet from the water. I looked to the top of the tree from which it must have come, but could see nothing. I refocused my attention on the book and knew immediately its origin.

It was a barely legible copy of *The Merchant of Venice*, so badly used that I had to turn many pages before I could make out

... I put this down on my list of things to worry about at some other time.

the full title. It was a volume from the works of William Shakespeare that Ralph had told me about years earlier – the Shakesbear clan's treasured heirloom, used by the matriarchs of each generation to instruct their offspring in the idiosyncrasies of the English language.

There was no mystery about where it had come from or how it had arrived. My mischievous friend Duffy had flung it out of his tree to attract my attention. That's good thinking, Duffy, I thought.

The tree was on the opposite side of the stream and I couldn't spot the little bear in the foliage, but I heard his shrill voice sing out, "Hark, I hear the footing of a man. Who comes so fast in the silence of the morn?"

Going along with the gag, I replied, "It is I, Shylock, come to enquire of your well-being and to collect my pound of flesh. Now get yourself down here and tell me what's going on."

Hark
I hear the footing
of a man.

From the back side of the tree came the clattering of disturbed bark and the cloud of dislodged debris as the cub came scrambling down from his perch. Duffy landed clumsily on an old dead branch, sprang to his feet and with a flourish and a proper Shakespearean bow, pronounced loudly over the noise of the rushing waters: "At your pleasure, sirrah, how may I be of service?"

"I seek audience with your leader. Ralph be his name. Take me to his presence." I said, entering into the spirit of the thing. "And here's your book back. You don't want to lose any of your collection." I placed the forlorn copy of *The Merchant of Venice* on top of a nearby stump.

"There's precious little of the set left," said Duffy. "I'll pick it up on my way back. Follow me." Using a convenient boulder, he bounded across the water to my side and headed upstream. For some reason, I thought we should be going the other way.

"I had the idea you lived in the other direction," I remarked.

"We used to, but we got flooded out. Had to move upstream. Grandpa's mad about it, too. Along with everything else." The cub was moving rapidly – faster than I could keep up. For five minutes I did my best to stay close behind him but finally I surrendered.

"Hey, take it easy, Macduff. I've only got two legs, you know."

I couldn't help but notice that the young bear had grown considerably since I had last seen him. When does a cub stop being a cub, I wondered?

"Sorry," he said, sitting down on the hillside. "A bit out of shape, eh? We've got some climbing to do, better take a breather." I sat down next to Duffy and lay back to relieve the weight of my backpack. I thought I felt a drop of rain.

"Dang," I grumbled. "Don't tell me it's going to rain again. Enough already."

"Oft a little morning rain foretells a pleasant day," said Duffy cheerfully.

"By the way," I said, "that little bit of happy poetry reminds me that in your note you mentioned the computer is broken. What happened?"

Duffy seemed embarrassed. "Dropped it out of the tree. Right on top of a rock in the crick. Busted to bits. It's done for. Sorry."

"No problem," I said. "It wasn't yours in the first place, remember? What did you do with the wreckage?"

"Put it on the seat of one of those bulldozers. Maybe that wasn't such a good idea. The next day I was up in the tree and I saw one of those sheriff cars down there. Sheriff was talking to the boss guy, writing stuff down on a clipboard. Next day the bulldozer guy had a rifle on the seat next to him, probably waiting for those two robbers in the Halloween costumes to show up." Duffy chuckled. "Ralph wants to put dirt into the gas tanks, but I talked him out of it."

"Where is Ralph? How come he isn't down here?" I began to get myself back into my pack.

"Gramps has had a lot of problems. Three months ago he got in a fight with a cougar. Then he had a run-in with some rednecks and a collision with a motorcycle. Mostly he's mad about those roads up there. He's really out of sorts. I'm worried about him. You'll see."

Duffy continued on upstream. When we reached a large log we crossed back across the creek, which by now was considerably narrower. The underbrush became denser. Duffy proceeded effortlessly up the side of the canyon, but I did so with difficulty, my backpack snagging on every possible obstacle. I was about to call out for mercy when Duffy finally stopped. The sounds of the water were fading in the distance as we reached a small plateau, a place of refuge where it was possible to stand upright without having to hang onto something for support. Duffy startled me by making a sudden popping sound with his lips. When I heard the reply from up ahead I knew we had finally reached Ralph's headquarters.

It was with just a twinge of trepidation that I stepped through the last barrier of huckleberry bushes into the presence of "His

Majesty." It was eight months, I think, since I had last seen Ralph and by all accounts he had been "out-of-town and off his feed" for some time. I sure didn't know what the result of an altercation with a cougar and a motorcycle would be or what sort of greeting I would get, but I was glad that my good-natured friend Duffy was there to run interference should I need it.

"Well, old man, you took your time getting here. Where's the beer? Sit down, we've got things to talk about." The greeting was brusque but about what I should have expected.

Ralph looked tired and his voice had a note of weariness to it. He was resting on the ground in an awkward position with his back to the hillside in a kind of semi-repose. He seemed to be favoring his right shoulder. Next to him was what I took to be the entrance to his cave. It was a fairly large opening, but not very deep. I could easily see the back of the cave in the dim light. Ralph waved his paw languidly in the general direction of a small rock, which I assumed was what he expected me to sit on. It pained me just to think about it. I looked about to see if there might be something more suitable just as Duffy reappeared, rolling a short log into the clearing. Where do these bears manage to come up with all these short logs?

"Thanks, Duffy," I said. "You're a very thoughtful young fellow."

I shrugged myself out of the backpack and took a seat on the upended log which was probably not much of an improvement over the rock.

"How's it going, Ralph?" I said, trying to sound cheerful. "You don't look to be in good shape. What's been happening?"

The old bear squinted at me narrowly. "You got any beer in that bag? I got a mighty dry throat."

I removed the six-pack and placed it on the ground beside me. I could see his spirits improve immediately.

"Duffy, bring a bottle over here and help me with it."

I watched in amazement as the next bit of ursine theatre unfolded. Using his mouth, Macduff extracted a bottle from the carton and carried it across to Ralph who grasped it firmly between his hind feet while the little bear twisted the cap. Then in a maneuver that I would have supposed was beyond the ability of a bear to execute, Ralph used his teeth to take the bottle from between his feet and, in one grand motion, threw back his head and emptied

the contents down his throat. Young Macduff quickly picked up the empty bottle in his mouth and put it back in the carton. Oddware Stumple would have been proud of him. When I recovered from my disbelief, it occurred to me that Ralph had resorted to these amazing contortions because he was not using his right front foot.

"You got something wrong with your paw, Ralph?" I asked.

"Punk kid ran into me with his motorbike," grumped the old bruin. "Just a flesh wound."

"Let me take a look at it," I said, going to his side.

"Never mind, it'll be alright,"

he said without much conviction.

I went around to his far side to have a look. I could immediately see that this was more than a mere flesh wound. It was a deep laceration in his upper right leg. Most of the fur in the vicinity was gone but it was just within reach of his tongue, which had allowed him to keep it clean. There was no sign of infection which was good.

My first thought (which had once appeared to me in a nightmare a long time back) was to load old Ralph in the truck and take him downtown to the vet. That old dream had me driving through town with the big black bear sitting in the back of the pickup with me suddenly surrounded by platoons of "authorities" – sheriffs, state troopers, swat teams, fish and game types – all with their weapons drawn and all competing for jurisdiction, jostling to see who could be the first to get the cuffs on me. I tried to list the number of laws and ordinances I would be charged with violating. Instead I simply shut down the mental image bank and put the whole thing out of my mind. Ralph and I would handle this ourselves.

"How long ago did this happen, Ralph?"

"I don't know. Quite awhile. It's getting better. It'll be alright. Duffy's taking care of me." I looked over at the young bear and it was clear that he was concerned, but before I could make suggestions about a course of action to aid his recovery, Ralph called out.

"Duffy, get me another one of those long-necks. The first one just barely wet my whistle."

Once again they went through the same routine, after which Ralph blinked several times and then belched loudly.

"That's an amazing routine," I said to Duffy. "It looks to me like you've been practicing it."

"We do. I swipe beer from the bulldozer guys. They're not very smart. They think they're stealing from each other. We've been doing it since Gramps got hurt. Trouble is they buy most of their beer in cans so Grandpa just bites them open. He's pretty good at that, too."

"You're pushing your luck, Duffy," I said. "Those guys aren't going to be fooled very long. By the way, what happened to the kid on the motorbike?"

"Last I saw of him he was doing his own imitation of a coyote chasing a rabbit, running down the road at his best speed," Ralph growled. "I thought my leg was broken otherwise I would have caught him and taken a bite out of his ass."

"How'd you happen to run into each other?" I inquired.

Ralph made an expression of disgust. "Well, it was just dusk. I was walking down an old road in the woods over near the golf course, minding my own business, when this punk kid comes free-wheeling down the hill and around the corner on his motorbike doing ninety miles an hour. I didn't even hear him coming and of course he couldn't stop. It was one hell of a collision. He went ass-over-teakettle, face-first into the scotch broom, then took one look at me and lit out running down the road.

His damned machine put this big gouge in my shoulder. I thought I was done for. Took me all night to limp home. Now that kid has probably noised it all over the place that this big old bear attacked him without any reason at all and that'll bring out the busy-body wardens with their dart guns. They'll be looking for this 'nuisance bear' so they can relocate him. And you know, I just had an idea. Maybe it wouldn't be such a bad thing if I did let them relocate me. I've about had it with this place anyway. It's just plain getting too crowded and too dangerous around here." Ralph seemed exhausted from the effort of telling the story.

"What happened to the kid's bike?" I asked.

Ralph's expression brightened at the question. "I guess the adrenaline was running pretty good," he said. "I bit holes in both his tires and then bent the whole damn thing right in the middle. That kid will need a new machine before he makes another trip around here. Trouble is I loosened up a tooth and burned my foot on the muffler while I was doing it." He held up his paw and showed me an ugly scar. "Get me another beer, Duffy."

I suddenly remembered the sandwiches I had prepared that morning. "You guys like salami sandwiches?" I asked.

"Does a bear shit in the woods?" asked Ralph, pointing his nose at the sky, his whole body shaking with spasms of mirth. At least I assumed it was spasms of mirth – I had never seen this reaction before. In any case, it was good that the old fellow was beginning to cheer up. The telling of his recent misfortunes had clearly been difficult. I wasn't sure whether the change was brought about by that last beer or the anticipation of something to eat.

I produced the four sandwiches from the backpack and gave two of them to Ralph. Duffy and I had one apiece. "That's cool, Dude!" said Duffy excitedly.

"You get two, Ralph. You're the biggest."

"That's good thinking," Ralph said

with a grunt. "You spared me the trouble of having to take it away from you."

I wasn't sure just how one goes about feeding a sandwich to a bear. Duffy saw my hesitation and said, "Just throw them on over, man. Bears only eat with their hands in cartoons."

I did as I was told, throwing one down at Duffy's feet and tossing the others in the direction of Ralph. In an instant the bears had ripped off most of the plastic wrappings and were wolfing down bread, meat, bits of plastic, dirt and debris. All this before I had even finished unwrapping my own sandwich.

"Help me with this beer, Duffy," said Ralph, loudly licking his chops. "Then have one for yourself. You have one, too, old man. There should be one left there."

"Gee, thanks," I said with what I hoped was enough irony to register on Ralph's tiny conscience. "You're too kind." Nevertheless, it made me glad to see that Ralph was showing signs of his old self-centered importance.

"Duffy tells me you've had trouble with cougars. What's going on?" I asked. I should have waited until Ralph was finished eating his sandwich. His diction was difficult to decipher under the best of circumstances and with his mouth full it was impossible. Whatever his answer was, I couldn't understand it. I held up my hand. "Finish your eats first, Ralph. I'll wait," I said.

We sat in silence for the half-minute it took the bear to devour his "meal" and drink his beer. "Damn cougars are not as much trouble as those land developers," Ralph grumbled. "Nobody cares if you kill a cougar, but you try to eat a land developer and you're instantly in trouble. There's too many of 'em anyway. I'm beginning to know how the Indians felt way back. You kill one settler and the next week there's another wagon load of 'em coming on to take his place."

"Duffy overheard the big shots over there talking about what they're going to do next: waterlines, power lines, telephone lines, blacktop roads, big signs. They're even going to build a real estate office. I've got to get out of here." Ralph had talked himself into a state of agitation. He rose painfully from his position, then thought better of it and eased himself down again. "Damn, that smarts," he said.

"I've got some stuff down at the house you can put on that wound that'll help it heal up," I said. "I'll leave it in the box down the hill. You have Duffy pick it up. Can you remember that, Duffy?"

"Yeah, man, cool."

"We can't go anywhere around here in the daylight anymore," groused Ralph. "I'm sure we've been spotted a couple of times because we've seen more sheriffs and game wardens hangin' around the back roads lately. That's a bad sign."

"They're probably still looking for the guys in the bear suits that stole their laptop computer," I said by way of making a little joke. "Or maybe the dudes who are stealing the bulldozer beer." I suggested, giving Duffy a meaningful look.

"You talk to Grampa. He's the one makes me steal the beer."

"You know, Ralph, you're not on the developer's property," I said. "It stops about a quarter-mile back. They don't build anything down in these canyons, anyway. You're safe down here."

The old bear looked at me with puzzlement. "You don't seem to realize the problem. As soon as houses go up around here you get cars, kids, dogs, motorbikes. You remember when you were a kid? You were out exploring all summer long. With your dog. It's just a matter of time until we're discovered. Try to get a few meals out of a garbage can and WHAM! you become a 'nuisance bear' and the jig is up. No, there's no way bears can live a quarter-mile from people without big trouble. Sometime you can visit with carefully selected members of the species *homo sapiens*, but there's no way you can live among them."

I think Ralph was paying me kind of a left-handed compliment. I guess I was one of those "selected" few who my friend could tolerate. The thought took me back to the day I met Ralph for the first time when I was totally convinced that I was about to become his lunch. That berry patch was less than a quarter of a mile from where I lived, but back then there were no other neighbors for long distances in any direction.

I tried to think of other reasons why Ralph should stay where he was, but knew full well that his arguments were far more reasoned than mine. I was trying to keep him in the neighborhood simply for my own selfish reasons – as a form of entertainment and as a source of whimsical sayings for my sign down on the highway. Ralph was thinking of survival. His very life could easily be in jeopardy. It was a lopsided equation.

"Hey, you got any more beer in that bag?" growled Ralph. "I'm getting a parched throat from all this talking."

"I've got another six-pack in the truck," I said. "It was too heavy to carry both of them down here. And there's no way I'm going up there to get it. You'll just have to stay parched, Ralph."

"I'll send Duffy. Hey, Duff, run up there and get the beer out of the old man's truck. We don't want it to go to waste. You got your truck locked?"

"No, it's not locked. Can the cub get the door open?"

"Never was a bear born that can't get a car door open," said Ralph with a chuckle. "If need be he'll just pull it off its hinges. Or take a big rock and bust out a window."

I was fairly sure that Ralph was pulling my leg, but just in case, I confirmed with Duffy that he could, indeed, get into the truck without damaging it. He set off up the side of the canyon, apparently taking a shortcut since he headed in a different direction from where we came in. "Be back in a jingle, man. Stay cool."

Ralph got slowly to his feet and limped around the small entrance area to his cave, making several circuits before seating himself again with his back propped against a small tree.

"It's getting easier," he grunted. "I had a bad time there for awhile. If it hadn't been for Duffy I might not have made it. He brings stuff for me to eat. Then that damn rainstorm flooded us out of our old cave. This new one up here doesn't amount to much and it's too easy to see. Anyway, summer's coming on and, like I say, I'm gettin' out of here." Ralph was peering at me intently. "And I'm going to need your help."

"What do you mean?" I asked. Here was a new development, this curmudgeonly, surly, self-sufficient old bear asking for help from me?

"What's up?"

"Well, last winter before I had the run-in with the rednecks and the motorbike, I was visiting friends and relatives down beyond the golf course. You probably know the area. Most of the old trees are gone so there's nothing but second-growth stuff. Developers haven't got there yet. Anyway, I ran into Rupert the Rummager down there. They call him that because he's always digging around in the garbage dump. He's a distant cousin of mine who lives up in the Skok Valley. Rupert's got a friend named Lucy Slowfoot who used to live with a toothless old boar bear called Pixley Poomer. One summer Old Pixley was charged with 'nuisance behavior' down around Hoodsport so the wardens 'darted' him and took him off up into the national park somewhere and turned him loose. That was all quite awhile ago."

Once a bear gets hooked on garbage, it's all over!

Ralph shifted his position gingerly and carefully scratched his wounded shoulder.

"Anyway, like most nuisance bears, Old Pixley started off just taking a little bit of garbage now and then and the first thing you know he was hooked on the stuff. Then it got so he couldn't stay away from it. He was tipping over cans, scaring the dogs and running the cats up into the trees. When that happens housewives get nervous and call the sheriffs.

"Now, if you leave this kind

of matter to the sheriffs they'll come out and shoot the bear and most everything else they can find. Sheriffs like to shoot things and when they shoot a bear, I guess they don't have to do a lot of paperwork like they have to do when they shoot a person. But, as I understand it, the sheriffs are required to call the game wardens and the wardens use dart guns. Shoot a dart into your ass and send you into a big sleep. You have nice dreams and when you wake up you've got a collar around your neck with a radio on it and you're bouncing along in a big barrel in the back of a truck on your way to some place way out in the middle of God-forsaken nowhere. You wouldn't believe what those wardens do to you when you're unconscious."

Ralph saw that I was about to interrupt him.

"Now, mind you, I've never been darted. I'm just telling you what Lucy told Rupert, so this is sort of hearsay, but I don't doubt for a minute it's true."

"What do they do to you when you're unconscious, Ralph?" I asked.

"They measure your collop, damn it! THEY MEASURE YOUR COLLOP, is what they do. What business is it of theirs how big your collop is? And they do a lot of other stuff, too. It's a damned indignity." Ralph had worked himself into a state of agitation

How would YOU like to have your collop measured?

173

which reminded me of some of those old political tirades he used to subject me to. When Ralph gets himself lathered up with his own rhetoric, he tends to forget his physical ailments, which is good if one can withstand the mental assault.

I sought to calm the old fellow. "I'm not sure you know what collop is, Ralph. Collop is fat. Those wardens measure your fat to find out if you're getting enough to eat. They measure everything – the length of your tongue, your teeth, nose, ears – the whole business. They punch a hole in your ear and put a tattoo on your butt. When they let you loose in the national park you become government property. For all I know you get a social security number, too."

"They try to catch me, I'll show them how fat my collop is," he growled.

Ralph was up on his feet now, stalking around his veranda, not even showing much of a limp. "Where in hell is that Duffy? He's been gone long enough to get to town and back."

"You forgot to tell me about your run-in with the rednecks, Ralph. What was that all about?" I asked.

"That was way back last fall over in one of those cut-over flats this side of the health resort. I'd been hunting bugs since most of the good berries were gone. Got into a good bunch of late grasshoppers – those big ones that make a lot of noise when they fly. Sometimes in a good season you can jump a bunch of 'em all at once, get several under each paw. Then the trick is to get 'em in your mouth without lettin' them get away. They're mighty good tasting. Like chicken, not that I eat chicken much. Anyway, I let my guard down, concentratin' too much on the grasshoppers and didn't hear these two dudes come over the hill, each one carryin' a double barrel shotgun. Must have been hunting grouse or pheasants.

"Of course, as soon as they saw me they both let fly. They were pretty good shots too, because I think they got me with all four loads. Fortunately, by then I was in overdrive, probably just about outrunnin' the shot, headin' for the woods. That bird shot doesn't penetrate into a bear's hide very far when you get some distance on 'em."

"I can imagine the braggin' those two dudes did when they got back to the saloon. 'Bagged a huge bear we did. Tracked him by a trail of blood all afternoon but he got away.' Anyway, any dang fool that would try to shoot a full-grown bear with bird shot can't be too bright. Just shows the caliber of people live around here nowadays. Duffy picked all the lead out. Itched to beat hell, though."

I was about to quiz Ralph for more details just as Duffy reappeared. He came racing down the hill with the six-pack of beer in his teeth, scattering a flurry of muddy topsoil before him.

Birdshot won't penetrate a bear very far ya' know.

"Hey, hold on there, kid. What's all the hurry about?" asked Ralph. "What's chasing you?"

"There was a sheriff up there looking all around your truck," said Duffy breathlessly. "He was writing stuff down and talking on his radio. I had to wait a long time before he got done."

"He didn't see you, did he?" asked Ralph with concern.

"No, I'm pretty sure he didn't. I stayed behind a tree, pretty far away. He walked all around the truck, looking at the ground. Took down your license number, too," Duffy said, his eyes wide.

"See what I'm telling you? These guys are closing in on us. We got to get out of here. Did the cop leave?" asked Ralph.

"Yeah, I waited a long time to make sure he wasn't coming back. I got the beer, too." said Duffy proudly.

"Good boy, Duff, you've got your priorities right. Now pop one open for me," said Ralph. "Let's all sit down here now and listen. I have a plan." He turned and peered at me intently. "This is where your help comes in."

Now what is this crafty old bruin about to get me into, I wondered? With memories of that sign deal we had made years before coming back to me, I resolved to be on my guard.

"I want you to drive me up to the park," said Ralph in a matter-of-fact way. "Relocate me, before I get darted and tattooed. Duffy can come, if he wants to, but I've got to ditch this place.

"Here's the deal."

CHAPTER TWELVE
We Put the Plan in Motion

Ralph's idea was that I would drive him down close to the south entrance of the park where I would turn him loose on an old logging road just outside the park boundary. Then he could look for Old Pixley Poomer, who was supposed to be working around there somewhere near the Staircase campground.

"What do you mean he's working down there?" I asked. Ralph proceeded to tell me about the "job" that Old Poomer had, sort of, on the payroll of the National Park Service. He said that he got the information from his friend Lucy who swore it was true. She said that after Pixley was darted and taken to the park he still couldn't kick the habit of digging around in garbage cans, but it soon became apparent to the rangers that the toothless old bumbler wasn't a threat to anybody and in fact, he became the biggest tourist attraction in the park. In the summertime he would show himself around the campground every once in awhile just to frighten the tourists who would rush to get into their cars to take pictures of the old humbug through the windows to send back to the folks in Omaha. The Staircase campground became the most popular place in the whole park and won prizes every year for doing the most business. During the off-season the rangers would feed whole bags of dog food to Old Pixley just to keep him around.

"The other campgrounds are thinking of hiring their own bears," Ralph said. "Lucy says there are employment opportunities down there."

I used every pretext I could think of to excuse myself from participating in his screwy plan. Nothing worked.

Our pow-wow continued on into the afternoon. It began to drizzle, driving the three of us into the dryness of the cave. It was close quarters with all three of us inside, until finally Duffy got bored with all the talk and said he was going back up his tree. He told Ralph to let him know when he made up his mind about what he was going to do. This made the conference less crowded but, by now, Ralph had finished all the beer and was slurring his words badly; I was having difficulty understanding what he was talking about.

His conversation turned to maudlin reminiscences about the "good old days" when a bear could call his life his own. Back when the only real danger a bear faced was hunters with their packs of dogs and their big old steel traps or once in awhile, a cougar whose mother hadn't taught him about bears.

Nevertheless, I learned that Ralph was completely serious about wanting to leave so I gave up trying to dissuade him. His mind was made up. He told me that if I wouldn't take him down to the park, he would walk. He said all the dangers of that kind of travel were no worse than the danger he faced living where he was.

I asked him why he didn't just get himself designated as a nuisance bear and have the wardens transport him to the park.

"Too risky," Ralph mumbled. "Sometimes those rangers get the dart gun dose too strong and then it's bye-bye forever. Not to mention all that other stuff: the collar, the radio, the collop business and the tattoos. I say the hell with it. I'd rather walk."

I could see that Ralph had worn himself out and was getting sleepy.

"I should think our long friendship would go for something," said the bear wearily, "would'st have a friend? Then would'st first be one."

178

"Always the quotations," I said. "Who said that one?"

"Ralph, the bear said it." He lay down and curled himself into a ball. "Pick up the empties before you go."

I did as I was told, cleaning up all the refuse we had left around the cave entrance. As I left, I could hear Ralph snoring. Sounds just like an old man, I thought.

I hoisted my backpack and headed back down the hillside even though I knew there was a shorter way back to my truck. I needed to find Duffy to figure out what to do with old Grandpa. As I approached the bear tree I searched the foliage trying to catch sight of the cub. Since I knew which tree Duffy had his hideaway in I thought it should be easy to spot him in the branches. Not so. I didn't spot him until he let me spot him. He climbed out on a limb in plain view, waved and whistled (I didn't even know bears could whistle). "I'll be right with you," he shouted and I sat down to wait for him.

IF YOU WOULD
HAVE A FRIEND
YOU MUST
FIRST BE ONE

He arrived promptly but all out of breath. "I was just reading in a newspaper about a bear up in a tree in Port Orchard, right in the middle of a bunch of houses. Must have been one of those dumb Toonerville bears. They've got their brains all burned out with that meth stuff. What did you and Gramps decide?"

"We didn't decide anything," I ventured. "I was hoping maybe you could help me with the problem. You know the old guy better than I do."

179

Duffy settled down beside me. "Well," he said, "here's what I do know. Old Grampa is losing his vigor. You know, I have no idea how old he is. He doesn't either, for that matter. Bears don't much bother with keeping track of time. But he's 'lost a step' as your sports people say and those recent adventures with the motorbike and the cougar have taken some of the steam out of him. He's serious about wanting to go down to the park, and the more I think about it, the better it sounds to me. It'll be kind of like a retirement home to him. There's no hunters in the park. No packs of dogs, no motorbikes. And if what they say is true – about Old Pixel getting fed regularly for just hanging around a campground – this sounds like a neat way to live. I have this picture in my mind of old Gramps sitting around the campfire in the evenings, telling

adventure stories to the tourists. Kind of like Yogi Bear."

Duffy saw my surprise when he mentioned this idea. "Relax, it won't happen. You're the only human bean Ralph has ever talked to and he has told me a lot of times that it was a mistake."

"Human bean?" I asked.

"Sorry. That's how I used to spell 'human beings' before Grampa told me different. He says *Homo sapiens* can't be trusted. He says probably the only reason you haven't told everybody about him is that nobody would believe you."

180

"Well, that's partly true, but I gave the old devil my word when I first met him, and by damn, I've kept my word." I felt a touch of disappointment.

"Now he's afraid you're going to start writing stories about him," said Duffy.

"Well, if I do it will be long after he's gone," I said. "How come the old grump hasn't talked about this to me?"

"It's like I say," muttered Duffy, "he's getting a little soft."

I think it was this casual conversation with Duffy that finally made me decide to help the old bear relocate. Even a bear needs some peace and quiet in his dotage.

"If I decide to help Ralph move to the park, how am I going to do it, Duffy?"

"Beats me," said Duffy. "You human beans are supposed to have all the smarts, you figure it out. Take him in the truck, I guess."

"Do you know that we human beans have a law that says it's illegal for us to have unlawful contact with a wild animal?"

"What's unlawful about driving a bear around in the back of a truck?"

"I don't know, Duffy, but we'd find out quick enough if I tried it. I suspect it's even against the law for me to be sitting here talking to you."

"Which reminds me," said Duffy. "I think you'd better keep your eye on that sheriff dude. He seemed

181

mighty interested in your truck. He saw that carton of beer in it too, and I bet those bulldozer guys have been telling him about all the beer they've lost."

Duffy stood up and shook himself vigorously. "I gotta get going, dude. When you figure out how you're going to work out this bear-to-the-park deal, leave a note in our box down the hill and I'll let you know when it's safe to come up. We're going to have to get going soon. Won't be long, they'll be building houses up here."

I made my way back up the steep hill with difficulty and then through the brambles and underbrush to where I had parked my truck at the end of the gravel road. As I drove home, my mind was a turmoil of emotions.

First of all, I was disappointed that my old friend was going to leave. In spite of all our difficulties, I knew I would miss him. But more immediately urgent was how I was going to get him way down there to the park. It was close to forty or fifty miles by highway and much longer as the bear travels.

Years earlier, Ralph had recounted stories of his travails in trying to visit some of his kinfolk in an area much closer to home. I had no doubt that he could still walk that far, but with the increases in population and traffic since that time, his chances of making the trip safely were much diminished. There was no doubt in my mind that I would have to

You work out the details, I'm going to take a nap.

figure out a way to get the old boy down there.

I'd have to borrow a truck from somebody. My old pickup didn't have a cover on it and transporting a real live bear in the back of an open truck for fifty miles was out of the question. Just very briefly I toyed with the idea of having him ride up front in the cab with me. I had this mental picture of an old book I had when I was a very small boy — the story of the three bears, with mother bear in a dress and apron, wearing one of those granny hats with the ruffles around it. Maybe I could dress Ralph up like that and if anybody stopped me I would just tell them I was taking my grandmother to the dentist. Probably wouldn't work. People are smarter now than when I was a kid. Nobody would believe me. Anyway, a car seat was never designed to accommodate the size and shape of a nearly three-hundred-pound bear. Not even one who could read and write and talk politics.

As I drove myself back down to the house, I realized that I was very weary. A whole day in the company of a couple of bears - one full of beer - was an exhausting business. My mental processes were showing signs of wear. I'll work this problem out in the morning, I thought.

Alas, the morning did not bring a solution. It just brought more problems. I was sitting in my easy chair reading an article in the paper about a bunch of psychology professors with too much time on their hands, who had just published a study about Winnie the Pooh's mental problems and how they would treat him if they had the opportunity, when there came a knock at my front door. I answered the summons, and found, much to my amazement, a large, over-weight sheriff's deputy standing there. He had on those big, black aviator-type glasses that wouldn't let you see his eyes. As a matter of

183

fact, in all the time I knew this guy I never did see his eyes. I naturally assumed they were beady, as befits a person of his calling.

His greeting to me was brusque and businesslike. "Good morning, sir," he said without a smile. "Are you the owner of the pickup truck in the carport yonder?" He gestured across the road.

I resisted the temptation to make some quip about what part of the south he might be from. "Yonder" isn't a word used much around here. In fact, I had to suppress the urge to make a clever quip about this guy every time he opened his mouth. He was your stereotypical backwoods law officer with a big moustache, oversized

Is that your truck over yonder, mister?

belly, and self-important manner. He had more tools and gadgets hanging on his belt than a journeyman electrician. As much as I wanted to, I knew that making wise-assed comments about these matters would not be a good idea.

So I substituted a "what's it to you" with a "yes, sir, that's my truck. Why do you ask?"

"This truck was reported parked on a road in the Mountain Vista Estates development yesterday."

"Oh," I asked innocently. "Who was it reported by?"

"Actually, it was reported by myself," replied the deputy officiously.

"Must be true, then," I said, hoping this subtle quip wouldn't bring out the handcuffs.

"Would you like to step over to the vehicle with me?"

"Well," I said. "It would probably be better than standing here in the doorway letting all the hot air out of the house. Maybe you'd like to tell me what this is all about, Deputy, uh, uh." I was trying to read his name tag.

"Edd. Deputy Edd. Spelled with two 'ds'."

"That your first name or last?" I was thinking of that talking horse, Mister Ed.

"Last name. First name is Frederick."

Oh, has a nice ring to it, I thought. Fred Edd. I didn't let on I was amused. He'd probably heard all the jokes about his name already. I stifled the urge to make a clever comment about his mother.

We walked across the highway, around Fred Edd's patrol car to the back of my truck.

"I see you've got a bunch of empty beer bottles here," said the deputy ominously.

I was trying to think if it was unconstitutional for a policeman to look in the bed of somebody's truck.

"Yes, dang it, they're all empty. Drank 'em all," I said. "Forgot to take 'em out of the truck last night. I recycle, you know."

Deputy Edd seemed unamused. "They's been reports of beer thefts up there at the construction site. Guys runnin' the dozers report losin' beer. Your truck was seen up there. You got empties in the truck. Put two-and-two together. Mind tellin' me what you was doin' up there yesterday?"

"I'm a naturalist, officer. I do part-time environmental work for The Evergreen State College, studying the flora and fauna of the local

185

habitat with specialized work on wildlife and insects."

I was doing my best to sound like Oddball Oddwall and not succeeding. "There's an interesting colony of *Caribius nemorialis* up there," I said, making up a fancy name. "That's the common black beetle bug, you know."

I don't think Deputy Edd was taken in by my blarney. "I didn't think you science guys drank so much beer."

"Well, we do down at Evergreen. We've discovered that beer helps sharpen the thought processes."

The deputy was over at the truck counting beer bottles. "Yep, this is the number reported missing. I'm putting two-and-two-and-two together here. You got a receipt for this beer, maybe?"

"I've got it on good authority that those bulldozer people drink their beer out of cans," I said. "They shouldn't be drinking while operating heavy equipment, anyway."

"How do you know they drink beer out of cans, mister?"

I suddenly realized that maybe I was blabbing too much. Everything I said could be used against me. "Oh, I take walks up there. I see what they're doing. They drink lots of beer, all out of cans. Then they throw the empties all over the place. They are not good stewards."

Deputy Edd looked at me curiously. He was about to say something, then thought better of it. I think the word "stewards" may have thrown him off track. "What do you know about the theft of a laptop computer up there last year about Halloween time?"

"I know nothing about the theft of a computer," I said with indignation. "What kind of a person do you take me to be, Mister Edd?"

That slip of the tongue was quite unintentional and I knew it wouldn't help my case. I'm a terrible liar and it was time for me to shut up. The deputy was busily writing stuff in a little notebook.

"Well, I just want you to know," he said, "that we're going to keep a watch on you, mister. You will be well-advised to keep your nose clean. There seem to be a lot of coincidences here. More than meet the eye."

"Tell me, Deputy Edd. Have you checked my record? You find any felonies, any outstanding warrants? Am I wanted for anything?"

Edd was hitching up his tool belt and getting ready to climb back into his car.

"Not yet," he said. "But you can never tell when some people go bad. It's never too late. Age don't mean nothin' when it comes to criminal behavior. By the way, that there license plate is pretty dirty. Better get it cleaned off. Straighten it up too. Law says plates gotta be straight."

He started his engine and drove off down the road without so much as a "have a nice day."

That crack about old criminals was a very insensitive remark, I thought. I wondered if I had grounds for an age-discrimination law suit.

I tried to put the matter out of my mind and went about my business as usual for the next few days while at the same time considering ways of getting Ralph out of my backwoods and down to the park. I did observe that Deputy Edd and some of his colleagues seemed to be driving through the neighborhood more often than usual, but I pretended not to notice.

Day-by-day I watched for a signal from Duffy. I did remember to put the medicine for Ralph's wound in the box. It had disappeared, so I knew that Duffy had been down to get it, but two weeks had gone by without a signal. I drove up the hill one day to see what progress was being made on the "luxury estates" and I was disturbed by what I found. The roads had been graded and improved but not yet black-topped. Gleaming yellow fireplugs stood on alternate corners. A large concrete water tank was under construction. On a cul-de-sac, a huge computer-guided well drilling rig was grinding its way into the earth. A real estate office was taking shape.

Mister Edd was parked nearby in his patrol car, eating a hamburger and watching the digger dig. I waved but he did not return my greeting. Damn, I thought, doesn't this rural Inspector Clouseau have anything else to do?

I had begun to formulate a plan. I knew that even if there was a way to conceal old Ralph in the back of my truck, there was surely no way I could chance trying to sneak him past the beady-eyed scrutiny of Deputy Fred Edd. I would have to borrow my neighbor's small pickup truck. It had a canopy on it with tinted sliding windows which would conceal Ralph sufficiently so that only by close scrutiny would anybody know that he was back there. I could even cover him with a tarp if need be. Then, if Edd came snooping around, I would make him produce a search warrant, and if that didn't work, I could hit him with violation of the fourth amendment *and* an age discrimination lawsuit, a powerful combination of charges that I suspected he would wish not to face. I wouldn't let Deputy Dog see me in the little pickup anytime before the actual escape so that he wouldn't start tracking that vehicle, too.

The truck had that little sliding window behind the seat so I would even be able to communicate with Ralph during our trip. I might need to comfort him and calm his fears as we drove along. The more I thought about it though, the more it seemed that the situation was likely to be exactly the opposite. I'd been doing a little research on wildlife laws and had discovered that it was some kind of gross misdemeanor in our state for a citizen to be consorting with wild animals of any kind, even a snake or a gopher. Whether it be for moral or immoral purposes didn't seem to matter. I don't know why, but I had the feeling that Mister Edd was familiar with this covenant, too.

Several more days passed and finally, one rainy morning, I saw the signal in the stump. I hastened up the hill and found a "Duffy note" in the box. It was scrawled in purple crayon in big letters on a page out of the writing tablet.

"Grmps betr come sun Duf" was easily translated to read: "Gramps is better. Come Sunday, Duffy."

There was a problem however. Was I supposed to come prepared to transport Ralph or just for another planning session? I decided to chance another trip up the hill in my pickup to clear up the confusion.

When Sunday arrived I was late getting started and it was nearly noon before I drove down the "street," which I learned from the shiny new sign was now to be known as "Romance of the Old Growth Trees Avenue," despite the fact that the area hadn't seen old-growth of anything for eighty-five years. Given a choice, I would have named it "Ralph's Road" or "Ralph and Duffy's Place" or some such, but of course I didn't have any input in the matter. Ralph and Duffy's sounded too much like a saloon, anyway, and would have diminished the upscale appellation of the "Mountain Vista Estates" business.

As I drove past the new real estate office I noticed a car parked next to it and what appeared to be a man wearing big dark glasses seated at the desk inside. I was startled to realize that it was my friend Agent Edd sitting in there. Apparently he had swapped his badge for a career in real estate. I didn't acknowledge recognition and drove on down to the end of Old Growth Avenue and parked. Before I went over the little rise, I could see through my rear view mirror that Edd had come out the front door of the office and was watching my movements.

I lost no time heading down the hill toward Bear Gulch hoping that Duffy was up in his tree keeping me under surveillance and that he'd be down in the canyon waiting to greet me when I arrived. He didn't fail me. Duffy motioned for me to follow him and, instead of heading upstream toward the cave that I was

familiar with, we went downstream to Ralph's ancestral cave where he and most of his forebears (!) had lived and where generations of bears had studied the works of William Shakespeare.

On the way down the tangled trail, Duffy explained that, as best he could gather, Deputy Fred Edd had been hired some months earlier to serve as a private security guard on the Vista Estates and then had worked himself into a weekend job as a real estate salesman. Edd, said Duffy, was a self-important and overly officious obnoxity (a word I'm still trying to find in the dictionary) and even when he was on official duty, making his regular sheriff patrols, he was always prowling around Vista Estates making life miserable for my bear friends.

"Grampa is ready to go, man, and so am I," said Duffy with feeling. "This place sucks, man. I'm outta here."

We had arrived at Ralph's cave. Fortunately the sun was high enough that it shed some sunlight inside, illuminating the interior. This "residence" was much superior to the temporary cave the bears had occupied during the recent flooding. Ralph came hobbling to the entrance, clearly still suffering some discomfort from the recent motorbike injuries, but I could immediately tell that his mind was preoccupied with other matters. For the first time I could remember he neglected to ask me if I had brought any beer. I was relieved, because I hadn't brought any, a condition that sometimes caused the old brute to become quite sullen.

Ralph got right down to business. "Come on in," he said brusquely. "If you want to sit you'll have to do it on the ground. The water floated most of our stuff out of here so we're all out of short logs. Sorry."

This was the first time I had ever heard Ralph say he was sorry about anything. Was the old rouge becoming civilized, I wondered?

I had to sit. There wasn't enough headroom to stand.

"Duffy, you get back up in that tree and watch for that salesman. I know he won't come down here, he's too lazy, but I want to know what he's up to."

Ralph turned to me and wasted no time letting me know that things in the back woods were going from bad to intolerable. "You got your plans ready? If I don't get out of here pronto, I'm going to have me a deputy sheriff for breakfast. It's going to be me or him. I read somewhere that there's only been one citizen done in by a black bear in this country in recorded history. But I got to tell you they're going to have another one if I don't get out of here quick."

Plainly, Ralph had not succumbed to the calming influence of civilization.

I outlined my plan and such was his desperate need to leave quickly that he didn't argue or quibble. Everything I suggested was okay. "Let's get going," he said.

"All right," I said. "I will be up here early tomorrow morning. Make it about six o'clock so we won't be bothered by Mister Ed; it's doubtful he ever gets up that early. I'll back the truck down as close as I dare to the edge of the canyon. It's a little black Nissan with a canopy. Got a lot of miles on it, but it'll do the job. Soon as you see me get the back door open, you come lickety-cut and jump in. Hunker down and stay down. I'll tell you when it's safe to sit up."

Duffy reappeared at the entrance of the cave. "Deputy Dog was snooping around your truck again but he's gone now."

"What about you, Duffy? You going to go, too?"

"Got to, man. Like I said, this place sucks. Haven't got any friends around here anymore. I'll try the park with Gramps."

"That's going to make things a bit cramped in the truck, but we'll make it," I said. "Just make sure you're on time. Might be a good idea, Duffy, if you would get up in your tree early so you can spot me when I come down the road."

"Cool, man. I got a straight shot right down Romance Avenue. I'll see you coming. Do you want us to synchronize our watches, commander?" he asked with mock solemnity.

"Never mind the jokes, Duffy, this is serious business," I said sternly.

"I think the boy has a point. What's six o'clock?" grumbled Ralph.

"Dammit," I said. "Why don't you both just sleep in the tree tonight? Watch for me when it gets light in the morning. If we screw this thing up, I'm not going to try it again. You'll be on your own. Deputy Big Shot down there is just itching to pin some kind of rap on me. He's sure I'm the one who stole that computer last year." I gave Duffy a meaningful look.

"All right," I went on. "I'm outta here. You guys know what you're supposed to do. Now for God's sake don't screw up."

"Cool, man," said Duffy. "Six o'clock."

"And, by the way," I said. "I may be wearing a disguise in the morning. Don't be surprised if I look different."

I clawed my way up the canyon to the truck and drove back down the "avenue" slowly, so as not to excite Mr. Edd, but as I approached the real estate office he popped out the door and was standing in the road. I brought the truck to a stop.

"Afternoon," I said cheerily. "You've taken a new job I see. Given up law enforcement have you?" I wanted to do my best to avoid confrontation, at least until I had those bears out of the neighborhood. But what I really wanted to ask Mr. Fussbustle was just how he expected to sell real estate to anybody while he was wearing those fearsome black glasses. Used cars, maybe, but not real estate.

"Mr." Edd was serious and unsmiling. "Just a weekend job, friend. I'm still on the department. Also I keep an eye on the development up here. Make sure they's no monkey business. Kids and others like to squirrel around in places like this."

"You're right," I said with equal seriousness. "We can't be too diligent about keeping monkey business under control."

"Thinkin' of buying a lot, maybe?" asked Edd. He did his best to muster the hint of a smile, but it was plain he was no good at it. "Got some nice parcels. We haven't got our advertising done yet. Want me to show you around? I could probably get you in on a good deal, bein' you're early and all and you're a friend of mine."

"Didn't know I was," I said with surprise. Me? A friend of his?

"I keep my two jobs separate; sales

and law enforcement. Two different things." I couldn't help noticing that Edd's gaze often seemed to stray toward the bed of my truck as though he might be looking for beer bottles. That, and the fact that he still wore his inspector's goggles gave me all the clues I needed to decide which career he favored.

"Been up studyin' your bugs, I reckon," he said with just the tiniest touch of sarcasm. "Them caribean memorials or whatever you call 'em."

It took me an instant to realize that he was talking about that cock-and-bull story I told the deputy about the beetle bugs.

"Yes," I replied earnestly. "Weather's a little cool today. They're not moving around much. I'm heading home." I eased the truck into gear. "Keep in touch, Edd."

"Say, by the way," he said. "This is still private property up here, ya know, and will be until the developers turn it over to the property owners. You might keep that in mind. We're puttin' a gate on the entrance."

Edd had just switched occupations again – out of sales, back into the law.

As I drove off I could see him through the mirror, scrutinizing me. Probably checking to see if my license plate was straight.

I headed home to work out my elaborate plans and to get rested up. Tomorrow promised to be a busy day.

CHAPTER THIRTEEN
A Close Run Thing

When I got back home I went right over to my neighbor's place to borrow his truck. He was his usual inquisitive self, which in this case he had every right to be, since it was his truck, but I had never told him anything about Ralph, the talking bear or any of my other adventures up there in my back woods. Since he wasn't anymore likely to believe me than anyone else was, I had to fabricate another story about why I needed a truck.

As I think I've related before, I'm not good at making up falsehoods. Like Duffy said in one of his quotations, which was doubtlessly stolen from somewhere else, "A liar should have a good memory." My memory is anything but good and getting worse as I approach the sunset years. I told Larry, my neighbor, that I needed to go down to Hunter's Farm to get a couple bales of hay for the goats, forgetting completely that I didn't have any goats. Since he wasn't about to let me get away with this, I had to backtrack and say the hay was for Pam's goats. Pam is my daughter-in-law and, very conveniently, she does have goats. I told Larry that Pam's truck was broken and then tried to get all this firmly in my mind so I wouldn't screw it up if I got dragged into court on some charge or other. Like consorting with bears, maybe.

Just for a minute, I toyed with the idea of inviting Larry to ride along with me because he is an expert at revising facts. Once, down by the boat ramp at the state park he represented himself as a big-shot lawyer so convincingly that he scared away a boater who had a perfectly good damage case against us involving a dented fender. Having somebody with me who could bluster around in a lawyerly way would be invaluable if I should run into Mister Edd again. Upon further reflection, however, I decided that it was just going to be too difficult to explain this whole bear business to Larry and there was no way that I was going to get him to ride in the same vehicle with a bear anyway.

After swearing on my sacred oath that I would clean out his vehicle and guaranteeing that it would be spotlessly clean before I returned it, he gave me a reluctant go ahead. I moved the truck to my carport for a quick morning getaway. Then I set about working out the details of what I sincerely hoped would be a successful last adventure with Ralph and Macduff.

I had told the bears that I might be in disguise because I still had the nagging suspicion that Mr. Deputy Edd, the super sleuth, was going to keep watching me until he caught me in some infraction of the law, or his version of the law at least. The man was tenacious. I intended to tell his boss, the county sheriff, the next time I saw him that he had a real bulldog on his staff and he deserved promotion, preferably to some other jurisdiction. I hoped that Edd's Monday morning shift didn't begin as early as six a.m., but I wasn't taking any chances. A strange-looking driver in a strange truck should throw him off the track.

As usual, I hadn't thought the disguise business through sufficiently so I had to scrounge around to find a convincing get-up. A good disguise should start with a hat, and I had plenty of hats. I could go as a member of the French Foreign Legion, the British Admiralty, a Turkish potentate, a ship captain, a Swiss mountain climber or a bond salesman. After reluctantly deciding that these were likely to attract too much attention, as would a straw skimmer, a top hat or a derby, I finally settled on a cheap wig, a straw hat and a Groucho Marx nose attached to my own sun glasses. Figuring that the regular Groucho horn-rimmed glasses and moustache might be too obvious, I ended up looking like a cross between Groucho *and* Harpo. The straw hat added a down-home touch. If it didn't fool Fred Edd it would sure confuse the hell out of him.

I set my alarm clock for five a.m. so I was sure not to oversleep and then woke up every half-hour all night long waiting for it to go off. I was on the road at ten minutes to six with one of those blue tarps in the back to cover the bears if need be. At the last minute I decided to wear my big coat so I could turn up the collar to partially hide my face.

I quickly realized that I should have made a test-run with my disguise because with all my stuff on I could barely fit into the truck. I had so little headroom that I had to keep hunched over. If I dislodged the hat, the wig came with it. I began to think perhaps I had overdone the disguise just a tad. Oh well, I thought, as soon as I'm out of Deputy Edd's jurisdiction, I can take it off. Then I remembered that his jurisdiction extended all the way to the national park, I calmed myself by thinking that it was still much too early for Mr. Edd to be afoot.

It was but a five- minute drive to the rendezvous and I hadn't seen a sign of life along my route. Reaching the end of Big Tree Road, I made a U-turn and backed to the appointed loading spot.

As I climbed from the truck, my hat caught the top of the door and stayed behind on the seat with the wig. I saw Duffy, perched in the tree, watch in disbelief as I hastily restored myself. He was clearly puzzled by the man with the big nose in the big coat and seemed unsure if this was really the beginning of the great escape. I opened the tailgate of the truck and signaled for him to come down quickly. As he disappeared from sight I saw Ralph come lumbering over the crest of the canyon, moving at a fast clip which was good to see. His wounds must have healed. Right behind him came Duffy, running on three legs and carrying several volumes of Shakespeare under his arm.

I began to think I had overdone the disguise just a tad.

199

Ralph was having difficulty getting into the truck, so Duffy and I boosted him up and in. Duffy quickly followed, throwing the books in ahead of him. As I closed the gate and returned to the driver's seat (knocking my wig askew again) I realized that my neighbor's little truck was seriously overloaded. I calculated that I had about 450 pounds of bear in the back of a vehicle with weak springs and shock absorbers. Just one more complication.

"Lie down and cover yourselves with the tarp," I ordered through the little sliding window. "And if we get stopped anywhere you let me do the talking. You understand?"

"And it's high-ho, off to the park we go," warbled Duffy from under the tarp. "Merrily, merrily shall I live now, under the blossom that hangs on the bough."

"Duffy, the man said to shut up."

As I gently took the first turn to head down the hill, I realized that there was so much weight in the back of the truck I was going to have trouble steering. My front wheels were hardly touching the road.

"You guys get up toward the front as far as you can and hunker down. And for God's sake keep covered. That damned deputy has a nose for this kind of activity." I tried to avoid thinking of the nearly fifty miles of road ahead of us. The bears moved forward and things were better.

I reached the bottom of the hill and eased my load out onto the state highway. So far, so good. I adjusted my disguise in the mirror and began to relax. Two miles down the road, the first car I had seen all morning approached and as it passed I saw the driver's eyes widen with astonishment. What was that all about, I wondered?

I looked into the back of the truck and there sat Ralph with his head stuck out the side window like a big dog enjoying the streaming air flow, lips fluttering, slobber streaming back into our wake.

"God damn it, Ralph! You're going to screw up this whole deal before we even get started." I shouted. "That driver just about drove off the road. You keep out of sight. Everybody's got a cell phone nowadays and that guy's probably calling the cops right now. Duffy, make the old fart behave back there."

"Forsooth," said Duffy disappearing under the tarp.

I was beginning to get the hang of the erratic steering. The bears followed orders and for the next five miles all went well.

Then they began to go bad again. Ralph insisted on sticking his head through the sliding window into the cab of the truck so he could see where we were going, his hot breath fogging up the windshield in the process. "Dammit, Ralph," I shouted. "Get back there and lie down. I'm having enough trouble keeping this thing on the road even when I can see it." I shut the sliding window and scrubbed at the foggy glass with an old rag. The foggy glass became foggy, blurry glass.

In another two miles I noticed the steering becoming even more erratic and realized I'd better stop to find out why. I pulled to the shoulder of the road in the only spot available, which happened to be directly outside the fence of a waterside residence where there was barely enough room to get the machine safely off the road. Remembering to hang onto my hat as I alighted from the truck I discovered my right rear tire was just exhausting the last of its air and that Ralph was about to stick his head out the back window to see what was going on. And, as if this wasn't bad enough, from down the road I was horrified to observe the approach of a sheriff's car.

"Get down under that tarp," I hissed. "Both of you. And don't move a muscle. We're in big trouble. There's a sheriff coming."

"I wonder what a sheriff tastes like," I heard Ralph grumble as his head disappeared back inside the truck.

I busied myself around the backside of the truck, examining the tire as I heard the sheriff slow down. I caught a quick peek and determined that, as expected, my old nemesis, Fred Edd, was across the highway peering at me through his black lenses.

"Need any help there friend?" he called.

I was careful to keep my head down to avoid eye contact. The last thing I needed was Edd getting close enough to make out my phony nose. Why hadn't I taken the damn thing off after I had gotten down off the hill? I've got to bluff my way out of this now. I thought, counting on Deputy Edd being much too lazy to get out of his car.

"Naw, just a little ol' flat, officer. I'll have the spare on in just a bit. No problem. Much obliged, anyway." I thought if I put a little "southern" in my lingo it would show him I could handle the situation. "If I need any hep I'll call my boy on the cell phone. He lives just up the road. He'll hep me. Thanks a heap anyway. 'preciate it."

"Looks like you got quite a load there. Watta ya haulin'?"

"Jest got a load of chicken manure here for my boy's garden. Ain't goin' far. I'll make it all right soon's I get the spare on." I noticed with relief that another car was approaching. The sheriff was going to have to move on.

"Well, good luck. Better go slow. You get another flat you'll be out of business." Ed proceeded down the highway and I breathed a heavy sigh of relief.

A loud snort came from the back of the truck. "What's this stuff about chicken manure?" grumbled Ralph. "And who's the boy you're going to call on the phone you don't have. You got it wrong, old man. You're not hauling chicken shit back here. What you're hauling is bullshit."

"You just better be damned glad that I don't start telling the truth, Ralph, or you'll be dog meat in no time. Duffy, see if you can't keep the old devil quiet." I was busily detaching my groucho nose from my eyeglasses just in case Edd decided to come snooping back.

I was very glad that Larry was the kind of fussy guy that made sure everything on his truck was in good order. This wasn't the time to find that the spare tire was flat (if there even was one), or that there wasn't a jack or that the lug nuts were rusted on, or who knows what else might have gone wrong. I worried needlessly. Everything was in good order and I set about changing the tire. There was just one more complication. When I was about half done, the homeowner came out of his house to see what was going on and I had to go into my "down home" act again for his benefit. I was glad I'd taken the nose off. At close range it was too obviously phony to fool anybody and it was too early in the morning to pretend I was going to a costume ball which was one of the cock-and-bull stories I was planning to use in an extreme emergency. I had just lowered the jack and was putting it away behind the seat when the little truck gave a spontaneous lurch caused by one of the bears shifting position.

"That's mighty active chicken manure you've got there," remarked the citizen behind the fence. I was mystified by his comment for a second or two and then realized that he must have overheard me telling Edd that I was hauling manure.

"I'm not really carryin' chicken manure," I said, thinking quickly. "I got a couple Hampshire boars in there I'm takin' down to Hunter's Farm. Bill wants to get his sows serviced. Didn't want to tell the sheriff. For all I know there's probably some law against haulin' hogs. Well, thanks for the use of your property." I climbed back into the truck, knocking off hat and wig in the process.

As I drove off, the homeowner watched me go. He seemed puzzled, no less so when Ralph waved at him through the side window.

"Damn it, Ralph. You better hope that guy can't tell the difference between a boar pig and a boar bear."

Five miles down the road we approached the tiny village that in its more pretentious days called itself Union City, but which had long since given up the idea of becoming a city and settled on just plain "Union." Under the best of conditions, it's hard to classify a tavern and a small store as a city. There isn't even a gas station there any more, so I couldn't get my tire fixed in Union.

I wouldn't have stopped there

anyway. Another sheriff's car was sitting in front of the Union City Bar and Grill. My heart sank until I realized that this wasn't Deputy Edd, but rather one of his colleagues. They probably had a donut rendezvous there in the mornings before setting out on their appointed rounds. I proceeded onward at my measured pace, keeping my gaze straight ahead. The last thing I needed was any kind of eye contact with another deputy sheriff.

For the next several miles we moved on at a steady forty miles an hour. Even the bears were quiet. In fact I realized that Duffy had been unusually quiet throughout the trip. I craned my neck to peer into the rear and I could see that he was sitting with his back to the front of the truck bed reading a book. "What are you reading, Duffy?" I inquired.

"*The Comedy of Errors*," replied Duffy with a note of mischief in his voice. "Otherwise known as 'Ralph and Duffy's Trip to the Park' complete with the usual alarums and diversions. Shakespeare could have done wonders with this adventure. What comes next?"

"We are now approaching the reservation," I said. "Which, as I think of it, might be a very good place to turn you two reprobates loose. From what I know about Indians, they have a special thing about bears. They used to think you were some kind of gods or spirits or some such. Had a lot of bears on totem poles."

"From what I've read in the papers," mumbled Ralph, "they also shoot bears when it's convenient. Take us on to the park, please."

"I need to go pee-pee," Duffy piped up. "I don't want to make a mess back here. You better stop pretty soon."

God knows Larry doesn't want you too, either, I thought.

"You'll have to hold it until we get through Hoodsport, Duffy. There's no place to stop along the highway," I said. "I'm going into the gas station in town and leave the flat tire, so you guys get down under that cover and don't make a sound until we're on our way again. You understand?"

"I'll understand much better when you go into the store and buy me two six-packs of beer," said Ralph in a voice of unusual clarity. "In long-neck bottles."

"Dammit, Ralph," I complained. "That's just about the last thing we need right now. No beer."

"Surely you haven't forgotten the statute about consorting with wild animals have you?" said the old bear evenly. "I could make an interesting scene in the middle of downtown Hoodsport, you know. It wouldn't take but a few minutes for the TV helicopters to get here from Seattle, if you get my drift. How does this sound: 'ELDERLY EX-SCHOOLTEACHER LOOSES WILD BEARS ON CITY STREET.' Details at eleven. Paints a pretty picture, don't you think?"

Perfectly in character, I thought. The old bugger would readily resort to extortion to satisfy his frivolous impulses, no matter that we all could be in serious danger of being discovered right there in the middle of town. Even though I doubted that he would carry out his threat, I wasn't going to call his bluff. If I could just get through another hour or two of this melodrama I would be done with talking bears forever. The prospect of liberation broke down my resolve against buying the beer, but I would definitely set conditions.

"All right, Ralph, I'll get your damned beer, but you're not going to have it until we get to where we're going. You get a few beers in you and you'll be hanging out the back of the truck mooning all the cars along the highway. I can't take the chance."

"Cool, man, let's do it," chimed in Duffy.

"And I'm keeping the beer up front with me," I said forcefully.

"That's against the law," said Ralph. "You can't have alcohol with you when you're driving."

"Since when have you become an authority on the law?" I asked. "You just get down and be quiet. And get yourselves covered up. I've got to talk to the service station guy."

I parked the truck far enough away from the gas pumps to avoid having my load of "manure" attract attention if it should begin moving around again and arranged with the attendant to have my tire fixed and ready for pick up when I returned later in the afternoon.

Then I crossed the highway to the general store, got the ordered long-necks and, on impulse, bought three sandwiches and some other snacks, thinking we might have a little farewell picnic when we got to our destination. God willing.

Right next to the general store there was a little ice cream shop where several small children and their parents milled around the sidewalk window. Just as I was pulling away from the service station I heard a piping scream from across the road. "Mommy, look!"

One of the children had dropped her ice cream cone and, clinging to her mother's leg, was pointing at us, her little face contorted in fear. I accelerated faster than I had intended to and by craning my head way around could see that Ralph had his head out the window again. "SAVE THE BEARS," he shouted to the assemblage of startled

Mooning motorists sounds cule to me, Dude!

207

townsfolk. I stepped on the gas, doing my best to "lay a patch" in my haste to get out of town.

"Ralph," I yelled. "One more dumb trick like that and this trip is over. The park rangers are right around the corner up here and I can deliver you right to their door. They won't even have to go looking for you. My God! Talk about your nuisance bears. You've gone way beyond nuisance. Sit down and shut up."

"Duffy," I pleaded. "Keep the old bugger quiet. We've only got a little more to go."

"I just saw a chance to do a little education among the children. No harm done," said Ralph without apology. "They need to know about the plight of the bears. Who better than me to teach them?" He sat down and put on his best expression of martyrdom. "We must get the word out to the children."

I was doing my best to get some miles between the bears and the children. Once again Duffy began to complain about the need for a pit stop.

"Alright, Duffy, we're heading for the hills now. We'll find a place on the way up."

"Better hurry, dude. I've about run out of time."

As I turned off the main highway onto the back road leading toward the hills and then to the mountains in the distance, I began to have vague twinges of regret. In twenty miles I would reach the drop-off point and there I would release my feral friends into the wilderness they sought so fervently, away from the disturbance of human turmoil and danger. It had been nearly eleven years since I had met Ralph in the berry patch and nearly three years since Duffy had appeared. I had been both blessed and cursed by the companionship of these two puzzling creatures and I tried to calculate how my life would be changed with them no longer a part of it. I made mental lists of reasons why I should be glad to have them gone; yet always, there seemed to be an equal number of reasons why I would miss them. My reverie was abruptly cut short by a piping voice from the back of the truck.

"Are we there yet, Daddy? Because if we're not there in about two minutes you're going to have a wet load of manure back here. Your friend Larry will not be pleased."

We were a bare two miles off the main highway. I prayed for a track or trail off the road where I could ditch the truck sufficiently to take care of Duffy's needs. My hopes were quickly answered. Off to the right were the remains of an old logging road with a copse of second-growth trees in the near distance. We bounced down this primitive trail faster than was prudent, careening through puddles and over ruts and rocks, tempting a blowout of tires and/or Duffy's bladder. I parked behind a small tree, stopped and quickly opened the rear gate. Duffy leaped to the ground and raced into the scotch broom.

"That was a bad scene, dude," he shouted. "You need to plan better, man."

"Ralph," I said. "You'd best go, too, while we're here. There's no more stops until we get to the park." As much as the old bugger hated to follow orders, he did as I suggested and, taking my own advice, I followed suit. As we all stood there carrying out one of

Are we there yet, Daddy?

Mother Nature's most primordial dictates, I couldn't help wishing there was a wildlife photographer there to record the moment. This could make the cover of National Geographic.

Without the need to "zip up," the bears were done before me and Ralph was soon over at the truck, sticking his head through the cab window and sniffing around inside. "Never mind snooping around in there, Ralph. You just get in the back where you belong. That stuff is for later." Ordering the old bear around like this was a gamble and I held my breath, waiting for the explosion. Nothing happened. He just hung his head, looking at me with his beady little eyes as though he didn't believe it himself. Off in the distance I heard what sounded like the siren of an emergency vehicle and in a minute a sheriff's car went on by at high speed, blue lights flashing, headed downhill. What's that all about I wondered, hoping he wasn't looking for us. At least the cop was going back from whence we had already come so we didn't need to worry about meeting up with him as we proceeded on our way. The road from where we were to the lake was very lightly traveled so I let the bears sit up and watch the scenery.

It was hard for me to realize that our journey was nearly over and especially hard to believe that we weren't being pursued by agents of some legal jurisdiction intent upon foiling my plans to get the bears to some safe refuge. Ralph seemed lost in thought in the back of the truck, barely noticing where we were. Could the old rascal be having second thoughts, I wondered? His head had dropped onto his chest and I thought that perhaps he had fallen asleep, which might be a good thing. I doubt he had gotten much rest during his last night up in that tree. The next time I looked, the old bear was stretched out on his back in the bed of the truck sound asleep. Duffy was crowded into the corner still trying to read *"The Comedy of Errors."*

"Hey, listen to this, old man," he shouted through the window. ... 'hair is a blessing that time bestows on beasts and what he has scanted man in hair he has given them in wit.' How come you ended up without either?" asked the young bear insolently.

"That's rather insensitive, don't you think, Duffy? Shakespeare wasn't right about everything, you know."

"Yeah, but he sure had something to say about everything."

Duffy was having trouble getting comfortable. Ralph was now completely splayed out in the bed of the truck, taking up all the floor space.

"Dang it. Gramps has got me all cramped-up back here. The old boy is plum worn out. I don't think he slept a bit last night. He was so sure you were going to chicken-out and not come pick us up. He wouldn't let on of course, but he's been plenty worried."

I had an idea. "Duffy, we've got a straight stretch of road coming up. As soon as I find a place, I'll pull off and you get up here in front with me. You'll have to hurry and if a car shows up, ditch yourself in the bushes until it goes by. Got it?"

"Got it, dude. That'll be cool, man."

Our transfer went smoothly, but I hadn't reckoned with the peculiar anatomy of a small bear when it comes to fitting one into a car seat.

His hind legs were too short to reach the floor, but when he was sitting up straight he was almost as tall as I was. This could be awkward if we should meet an approaching game warden or park ranger. I quickly took off my hat and wig and fitted them on Duffy, deciding that the effect, weirdly comical as it was, would have to do. I couldn't help breaking out in giddy laughter. Being so close to the end of our journey was affecting my judgment.

Duffy got a glimpse of himself in the mirror and went into convulsions, which I took to be bear merriment.

"I wonder if this is what a sasquatch looks like?"

"Pretty close," I said. "Except that sasquatches don't wear hats. Damn! I wish I'd brought a camera. Nobody's gonna believe this."

We were skirting the shores of the lake now, which forms the extreme southern boundary of the park. Since it was still early in the tourist season, I counted on very little traffic near the campground, but decided it would be foolhardy to go straight into the area past the ranger's toll booth. There might be a park aide or one of those high school apprentices on duty collecting entry fees and, quite frankly, I had run out of falsehoods by which to explain the reason why I was transporting a sasquatch across park boundaries.

Instead I planned to cross the bridge where the river runs into the lake. Then I would take the old logging road that follows Elk Creek over on the west side and drive up into the hills until I could find a suitable spot to unload my cargo. This territory gets primitive real quick, but it's not far enough from the campground that Ralph wouldn't be able to find Old Poomer or whatever his name was.

"Duffy, my boy," I said with feeling. "You are just about at your new home. Another couple of miles and our trip is over."

"O Captain! My Captain! Our fearful trip is done! The truck has weathered every rack, the prize we sought is won." Duffy was beaming, proud of his poetic offering. "That's not Shakespeare, you know."

"Walt Whitman," I said knowledgably. "On the death of Lincoln. The captain wasn't driving a truck, though."

"Poetic license," said the young bear, sagely. "It's close enough."

CHAPTER FOURTEEN
Journey's End

We arrived at the turn-off from the main road, crossed the bridge, and headed up the bumpy Elk Creek logging road. I hit the first chuck- hole a bit too fast and the little truck bucked violently. Ralph awoke with a start and from the back came his loud bellow.

"We've lost Duffy! Stop the car, the boy's gone!" He started to the rear of the truck and began fumbling awkwardly with the latch.

"Relax, Grampa, all is well. I'm riding up here with the captain. Our fearful trip is nearly done."

Ralph must have been in a profoundly deep sleep. He was clearly discombobulated. "Who are you," he asked angrily. "Where's Macduff?"

Duffy couldn't resist playing on Ralph's confusion. "I'm a sasquatch. The old man here offered me a ride. I'm an endangered species, so don't try to harm me. I'm protected."

Ralph began to get the joke. His beady little eyes penetrated the young bear's disguise. "Dammit, Duffy, you gave me a start there. Where are we?"

"Not far from our destination, I hear."

Recovering quickly from his confusion, Ralph slid a side window back and thrust his head through. "So, out of this nettle, danger, we pluck this flower, safety," he shouted to the wilderness. "'Tis ever common that bears are merriest when they are far from home."

"What's that all about?" I inquired of Duffy.

"Some more corrupted Shakespeare. But it's cool, man. Means the old dude is feeling better. Grampa celebrates his approaching freedom with lofty thoughts of better days to come."

"As long as I know he can speak plain English, I wish he would," I said. "With everything else I've got on my mind, I really don't have time to translate Shakespeare."

"Can I take this silly disguise off?" asked Duffy. "This cheap wig is mighty scratchy."

"Be my guest, boy. I calculate we're out of danger. Another half-mile and we'll find a place to stop."

Off to the right I could see the line of majestic, old-growth trees that marked the boundary of the park. On my left, endless acres of national forest land were carpeted by young trees in various stages of growth, none of them destined to reach the grandeur of their aged ancestors be-fore they became raw mate-rial for two-by-fours. Ralph's excited babbling from the back of the truck interrupted my thoughts.

"Oh wonder! How many goodly creatures are there here! How beauteous! O brave new world," came the deep, guttural voice from the back.

Duffy leaned close to me. "That's sort of from *The Tem-pest*," he whispered. "Miranda talking to her old dad, Prospero, as garbled by Ralph."

Another short stretch of pot-holed road brought us to a little-used track into the

215

tangled second-growth. Two hundred feet into this thicket appeared a clearing perfect to our needs. It was an old log staging area. There was lots of rotted sawdust on the ground and best of all, pieces of cut logs all around in perfect sizes for seats. A stage just right for our leavetaking.

Out of habit, I backed the truck in so that I could make a quick exit should the need arise. It was best to be wary when cohabitating with bears, even tame ones.

I had barely stopped the truck before Duffy was out running around the clearing in excitement, his nose to the ground, checking new smells.

"Duffy," I said. "Before you go running off somewhere, find us some short logs to sit on. Your Grandpa and I are going to have a little pow-wow here." I opened the tailgate of the truck to let Ralph out and got the bag of beer and snacks out of the cab.

"Right, dude. You got it." Duffy scampered off to the pile of debris and was soon back with suitable seats. "You shall be known as 'Short-log Duffy,' my boy. You're a marvel," I said.

"I'm going to scout out the territory, Gramps. See what's around here. I'll be back." Duffy took off at the run, his nose to the ground heading back out the little road we came in on. Ralph shuffled into the woods to relieve himself, sniffing the air as we went. That was considerate, I thought, since it would be perfectly natural and proper for a bear to attend to his toilet right there in our picnic ground. I wondered idly, if this old bruin, after so many years of hanging around the *Homo sapiens* he so professed to despise, was actually taking on some of their "civilized" customs.

As Ralph returned he was still testing the air for odors. "I can smell 'em," he said. "There's bears around here. We'll

216

soon find out if we're welcome."

I wasn't sure if I wanted to be around when this happened. The solitary nature of bears is well-known, especially among the males who are very territorial, and with the rutting season not too far off I had the distinct feeling that I had better not tarry here too long. If Ralph was encroaching on the range of another male of breeding age there was apt to be a big fight sooner or later to decide who was to be "top dog," or "top dude," as Duffy had once described it to me.

Since it was still a bit chilly in the early afternoon, Ralph and I settled down on the sunny side of the truck for what promised to be our final conversation. He neatly removed the cap from a bottle and handed it to me. I was touched by this small token of consideration.

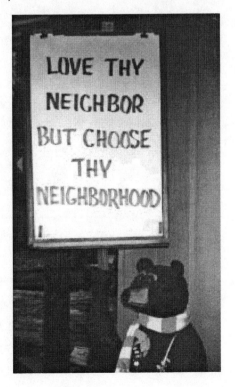

I noticed that not only had Ralph learned to get the bottle tops off with ease, he could now wedge the bottle between his claws and manipulate it skillfully enough to drink out of it like an old hillbilly drinking from a gallon jug.

"You've gotten pretty good at that, Ralph. I'll bet you could even hold a pencil if you tried."

"Let's not get into that again," grumbled Ralph. "But since you've brought it up, I don't think there's any need for you to keep that statue of me down at your place now that I've left the neighborhood. Give it up."

"We'll see," I said. "My readership might not allow it. But now that I think of it, everybody goes past my house so fast nowadays if a message is over three words long people probably can't read it anyway. Speed limit is forty. Not even the old folks go that slow anymore. Fifty-five is normal now."

"'Save The Bears' is three words. That's a good message. Leave it up all the time."

Ralph was opening another beer. "Maybe you could get Deputy Edd to sit out there and pinch a few of those speeders. That'd slow 'em down."

"I don't think Edd is much into catching traffic violators," I said. "His specialty is backwoods misdemeanors, like theft of beer and computers. I wonder if he's given up looking for us yet."

The answer to my question arrived in the person of Macduff who came zigzagging into our clearing at full gallop, still with his nose to the ground, tracking new smells.

"Hey, hold up there Duffy," yelled Ralph. "What's going on. What are you trackin'?"

"Trackin' wildlife, man. There's lots of good stuff around here. We got rabbits, weasels, foxes, coyotes, grouse, all kinds of piss ants. There's a big dumpster down at the campground, too. Man, we got everything! Awesome." Duffy was excited and out-of-breath. "I found some of Poomer's dog food, too. It's pretty good."

"Did you see Poomer?" asked Ralph eagerly.

"No, didn't see Poomer, but I ran into somebody who knows him. Her name is Peaches. She's Old Pixley's grand-daughter, she thinks. Calls herself Peaches Pixley–Poomer. I think I'm going to like it here. Gramps, Peaches says she'll show me around. Hey, you know what? That sheriff guy was down at the campground talking to the ranger."

"Oh, God, just what we need," I said. "Is he still there?"

"No, he left awhile ago."

"Any idea which way he went?" I asked.

"No, just out of the park, I think."

Ralph was already on his third beer. I hoped he wasn't losing his focus.

"Now listen, I said quickly. "If he should drive in here, you two get out of here as fast as you can go. Head for the underbrush. Get out of sight and keep going. Bon voyage and Godspeed. In spite of all our troubles, it's been good knowing you. Maybe we'll run into each other again somewhere. I'll take care of the deputy. As far as I know there's no law against sitting on a stump drinking beer. Now, don't take off unless you see his car coming. You understand?"

"Gotcha, dude," said Duffy, his eyes dancing with excitement.

Ralph belched.

To my great relief, Deputy Edd never appeared. I got out the snacks and the second six-pack, but we were mindful of our exposed position and maintained vigilance.

Being out of focus isn't so bad.

"Do you think your friend Peaches knows where old Poomer lives?" I asked Duffy.

"I think Peaches knows where everybody lives. She's cool."

"Well," I suggested. "As soon as you can, get your Grandpa down there and check things out. See if Poomer can find you a place to live."

Ralph was halfway to his mouth with his bottle. He fixed me with one of those baleful looks which let me know I had stepped over the line again.

"When I'm in need of a nanny," he said with feeling, "I'll let you know. I've told you before, but perhaps you need reminding, this experienced old bear has been finding his own living quarters for a good long time now and he can

Remember Ralph, a Fed bear is a dead bear.

continue to do so as long as it suits him. If I forget how it's done I'll come down and knock on your door. I know the way."

Ralph was right, of course. In the past few weeks I had been so closely aligned with the bears and their problems that I had begun to look at them as though they were helpless children. I was reminded that Ralph had told me not long ago that he was perfectly capable of walking down here to the park if I refused to transport him. I wondered idly how many of my recent problems with sheriffs and what-not were of my own making. The results of my own clumsy paternalism. After all, bears had been making their own way around here successfully since long before people like me showed up.

Yeah, but civilization was closing in pretty fast, I rationalized. Bears don't adjust to new challenges readily. What about the motorcycles and the shotgun-toting rednecks and the fast-growing housing developments? I was convinced that I had done the right

thing. My friends would be far better off up here in an environment more like what Ralph had known when he was a youngster
- away from high-speed traffic, beady-eyed deputy sheriffs and
domesticated dogs. The old fellow deserved some peace and quiet
after a long life of looking over his shoulder at "civilization"
snapping at his heels.

As we sat in ruminative silence on our short logs, Ralph
devoured an entire bag of corn chips and downed beer number six.
I could hear his stomach rumbling. My mind set sail again into
flights of fancy and wonderment. Years before I had asked Ralph
how old he was and he had professed not to know or care. I had
since learned that black bears can live to twenty or twenty-five years
and once again, I pondered on
how many seasons the old fellow had seen. He had plenty of
gray on his muzzle. He was
getting well along, I thought.
Will he be able to cope with
the vast spaces in his new range?
Those endless rows of hills and
valleys unfolding off to the west,
blending into the ragged peaks?
It was hard for me to visualize
Ralph being happy in the role
of a park host, hanging around
the campground to provide tourists with the occasional thrill of
seeing genuine wildlife up close.
Nor could I imagine him being

*I started with nothing,
I still have most of it.*

satisfied with a steady diet of government supplied dog food.

Out of the corner of my eye I could see that the old bear was in a state of deep contemplation. "You know what?" he asked, looking off into the distance. "I've always wondered what that 'ocean' thing is they talk about. Old Purple Lips Bartley used to brag about having seen it. I think I'll walk over there and have a look at it."

"My God, Ralph," I said. "Do you have any idea how far away it is?"

"No," he said. "But it can't be too far if that lazy old blowhard got down there."

"Probably forty miles as the crow flies, and you ain't no crow, Ralph. You got a whole lot of mountains between here and there."

"I'll send you a postcard when I arrive."

I decided there was no use in me worrying about the age and condition of the old coot. He was going to do what he wanted to do, which was fine with me. "You think you'll find somebody else to talk to?" I asked. "Somebody to talk English to, I mean?"

"God, I hope not," he said. "One experience like that is enough. From here on out I'll stick to my own kind." It looked to me like Ralph was down to his last beer. All the snacks were gone.

"It's probably about time I headed for home, old friend." I said. "I've got to stop and pick up the tire and get the truck back to Larry before he starts to fidget. It would be nice if you'd put all the empties in back of the truck, Ralph. If I run into super–sleuth Edd on the way home it'll give him something to fulminate about."

Duffy came loping into the clearing, all out of breath. "Hey, Gramps! I found Poomer, he wants to talk to you."

"All in good time, Duffy. You've got to say good-bye to the old man. He's leaving."

"Okay," said the young bear breathlessly. "When are you coming back?" he looked at me brightly.

"I don't think I'll be back, Duffy. This is going to be your new home now. Your Gramps thinks he wants to go over to the ocean. Maybe you can go with him."

"I'll have to ask Peaches."

"Well, that sure didn't take long," I said with surprise.

"Bears make friends in a hurry," said Ralph. "The kid's feeling his oats. He'll be alright."

Both bears were standing together awkwardly. As I prepared to get into the truck, I walked over and held out my hand to Ralph. "Good-bye, old friend. I'd like to tell you to keep in touch, but I don't suppose it would happen."

"Probably not," he said, touching my hand with his huge paw. He sat back on his haunches, his back feet crossed in front of him. I think he knew that I enjoyed it when he sat that way. I had told him once, a long while ago, in a rare moment of reflection, that it made him look pensive and wise and not quite so ferocious. Ralph spoke slowly, "How about putting up one more sign down there?"

"What kind of a sign," I asked?

"Just say 'RALPH SAYS THANKS FOR EVERYTHING.' That would be for all your readers. They've put up with a lot bad humor over the years."

The old bear scuffed at the dirt with his foot. "I guess maybe it could be for you, too," he said self consciously, meeting my eyes just for an instant before he looked away.

Before I could respond, I was suddenly enveloped in a bear hug. Duffy had pinned my arms to my side and planted a wet warm kiss on my neck. I could feel the faint touch of every one of his sharp adolescent claws on my back.

"Good night, sweet prince," he whispered, "and flights of angels sing thee to thy rest!" He released me from his grip and blinked several times. Could that have been a tear I saw in his eye?

"Hey, I know where that one's from, Duffy," I said, trying to avoid too much sentimentality. "That's Horatio talking to the dead Hamlet. But I'm not dead yet, kid. There's still life in this old carcass."

"Alright then, save the quote until you need it. And God speed your journey." Duffy stepped back alongside Ralph who was now on his feet. They each raised a paw in salute.

"Farewell, my friends. Take care of yourselves."

Ralph snuffled.

"Watch for the flag in the stump," said Duffy with a hint of mischief in his voice.

"You're joking aren't you?"

"Yeah," he said quietly. "I guess so."

As I drove slowly out of the clearing, looking back through the rear-view mirror, my vision was momentarily obscured by a large bush. When I caught a last glimpse of the bears they continued to stand, side-by-side, waving. My vision blurred. I was having trouble seeing the road. I rounded a slight bend and they were lost from sight.

Afterword

There was a lot of excitement in Hoodsport when I stopped to pick up my tire at the service station. People were still talking about the uproar earlier in the day when somebody had reported seeing a big bear in the middle of town. The kid in the station said there were cops tearing up and down the highway all afternoon, but apparently they never found anything. A little girl and her mother claimed to have seen the bear, but by the time the sheriff had finished grilling them about the matter they guessed maybe they weren't sure whether they had seen anything after all.

The rest of my trip was lonely and uneventful. When I arrived home and was cleaning out the truck I found the three volumes of Shakespeare that Duffy had taken with him. In his excitement, he had left them behind when he went tearing off to explore his new home. I still have them over there in the shop and I keep thinking I might take them back up to the park some day and leave them in that little clearing. Maybe he'd find them.

One of the books is *All's Well That Ends Well*.

THE END

ISBN 141201167-1